Jake turned to look at her. It was a mistake.

Bella's huge eyes were pleading, begging for his trust, and she was trying to blink back tears, biting down on her lip to still the trembling.

He abandoned his hard-won caution and pulled her into his arms. "Don't cry. Please don't cry! What I said was unforgivable," he declared against her hair, gathering her closer.

Bella lifted her head from his shoulder to search his face, and the anguish in his eyes was unmistakable.

She opened her mouth to accept his apology and heard him groan, his head dipping as his lips stopped the words in her throat.

His kiss was raw passion. Bella returned it— because this was what she'd been born for. To be his love, and only his.

DIANA HAMILTON is a true romantic and fell in love with her husband at first sight. They still live in England, in the fairy-tale Tudor house where they raised their three children. Now the idyll is shared with eight rescued cats and a puppy. But despite an often chaotic life-style, ever since she learned to read and write Diana has had her nose in a book—either reading or writing one—and plans to go on doing just that for a very long time to come.

Books by Diana Hamilton

HARLEQUIN PRESENTS®
1956—THE MILLIONAIRE'S BABY
1998—A HUSBAND'S PRICE
2015—THE BRIDE WORE SCARLET
2041—THE UNEXPECTED BABY

PROLOGUE

CHRISTMAS morning.

Bella leaned towards the mirror and stroked bright scarlet onto her lush mouth. A flag of defiance? Or an attempt to remind herself that she was still alive?

She recapped the lipstick and dropped it into her bag, then shrugged a soft leather jacket over the misty-heather sweater that matched her worn denims. She breathed irritably through her nostrils as her hair caught beneath the collar. Grabbing the long, silky black length of it in both hands, she secured it punitively in an elastic band.

It had once been her trademark—or one of her trademarks. Her silky jet hair, her lush scarlet mouth and the startling contrast of water-clear silver eyes had earned her the envied, yet oddly unenviable position of top photographic model of the decade.

A position of make-believe, of clever camera angles, exotic backdrops and the wizardry of the make-up artist—a position she'd gladly jettisoned when she'd married Jake. Preferring reality, as she'd perceived it then. The reality of being the wife of one of the most successful financial brains to work in the City, the sexiest, most charismatic, strong-minded man she had ever met. Jake Fox.

But the reality had been his, not hers. The real world had proved a hard place to live in when his reality had been his inability to give her what she wanted.

They had met and married in a breathtakingly short space of time. For him, she now knew, it had been lust at first sight. For her something different—so different that it meant a meeting point was impossible. She pushed that thought out of her head.

It was over. She had to keep that stark reality to the forefront of her mind.

She wouldn't think about anything else—the might-have-beens or if-onlys. Not now. Not until she could begin to hope to cope with it.

Snatching up her hastily packed case, she walked from the bedroom where memories of their lost and glorious passion seemed to echo mockingly from the very walls. She dared not risk a backward glance because if she did she feared she might change her mind and stay until he decided to come home, then beg for the chance to try again, and resign herself to a life of shattered dreams.

But she had too much self-respect for that. He had proved himself incapable of giving her what was her due. She couldn't allow herself to live with that.

Her chin lifted with stoic determination as she walked through to the elegant sitting room, avoiding the state-of-the-art kitchen where last night's celebration meal was cold and congealing in delicate bone china serving dishes.

Her fingers were shaking as she took the note from her bag. She'd written it in the early hours, after he'd walked in unexpectedly on her and Guy; after that blisteringly savage word he'd thrown at her; after he'd walked out to heaven only knew where.

It was to have been their third wedding anniversary celebration, and it had turned into a wake.

When he'd phoned from the States four days ago she'd begged him to wrap up his business meetings and get home for their anniversary. A quiet celebration for two. She'd told him they had to talk and find a way through to each other. His tone had been gentler, more loving than she'd heard it in ages, when he'd assured her he'd be home in good time—as if he, too, knew they had to cement the cracks instead of blindly papering them over; as if he too needed to draw closer, reaffirm their vows.

But he hadn't come. All day she'd waited, made preparations, planning the perfect menu, choosing his favourite wine, dressing herself at last in the little black silk creation he always said made her look sexy enough to short circuit his brain. All the time listening, ears straining for the sound of him walking through the door, her eyes flicking repeatedly to her tiny gold-banded wrist-watch, her pulse rate quickening with mounting anxiety.

By ten she'd just about given up hope, given up entirely on the spoiled meal. And when she'd heard the phone ring out half an hour later she'd picked it up, almost sobbing with relief. She'd been convinced it was Jake, letting her know he'd been delayed, apologising, letting her know he was on his way.

When it had turned out to be Guy Maclaine, business associate and long-time friend, calling to wish her merry Christmas and tell her his wonderful news, she'd gone to pieces, angry tears flooding down the phone lines because Jake had obviously forgotten his promise to be here. And because her relationship with Guy went back years, was very special, he'd come straight round. And half an hour later—wouldn't you know it?—Jake had walked in.

By then, of course, it had been too late.

She propped the note against the empty wine bottle on one of the glass-topped tables where he would be sure to see it—if and when he returned. It, the bottle and the single glass were the only discordant notes in what was otherwise a perfect room. It took some doing, as much courage as she had, because that farewell letter was so final. It ended their marriage.

But she did it. She had no real choice. And took several moments to compose herself, standing by the great sweep of the windows that looked out over the Docklands development.

Everywhere, as far as the eye could see, amidst the sprawling tense unseen family gatherings, then a stiffening of her spine. This was the worst Christmas Day she had ever had to face. But she wouldn't think about it.

Bella took up her case and walked out.

CHAPTER ONE

DECEMBER 23rd. Almost a year later.

'It seems a long way to come for a few days' break,' Bella ventured, staring through the afternoon murk at the towering hillsides. Now she knew why this range went by the name of The Black Mountains!

'Nearly there, so stop grumbling!' Evie countered blithely, changing gear as they left the road for what looked like a sheer mountain track. 'It's going to be fun, I promise. Better than being cooped up in that London flat of ours for the entire holiday.'

Fun? It was a bitter reminder that the past year had been anything but. Just work and more work, taking her position as head of the agency's New Accounts section so seriously that over one of their rare, leisurely lunches Guy had warned her, 'Sweetheart— never mind everything else we've got going for us— I'm talking as your boss now, and I'm telling you to slow down.'

He'd taken her hand across the table, stroking it softly, his dark eyes concerned. 'I know life can be a bitch, and things aren't going your way right now. But working yourself to a standstill won't help either of us. You're in danger of pushing yourself into a physical breakdown.'

It was a view shared by Evie. Not that she'd ever come right out with it, but it was there in her eyes.

In the space of twelve months Bella had become a dedicated workaholic, using every spare minute, not allowing herself time to brood. Was that why Jake had worked so hard? To stop himself thinking about the way their marriage had been slowly unravelling, falling apart? Had he found their relationship unfulfilling right from the day he'd woken up to discover his lust had been finally slaked and there was nothing else left?

Her breath caught. She swallowed the lump in her throat with ferocity. She wouldn't let herself think about it. Or him. Ever.

It would be a long time before she would be strong enough to take out and examine just what she had lost—contemplate the disintegration of precious dreams, the slow and devastating demise of the expectations that had turned into a nightmare, without falling apart.

'It will be different,' she said. Her voice was soft as she glanced affectionately at her sister, watching the way those bright blue eyes narrowed as she concentrated on the increasingly steep and narrow track ahead, her dark curls clustering around her pretty, plump face.

This break—a week in a rented holiday cottage in the Welsh mountains—had been Evie's surprise Christmas gift. Even if Bella would have preferred to pretend Christmas wasn't happening and take enough work back to the flat she had shared with Evie since her marriage had fallen apart to keep her occupied until she could get back to the office early in the New

Year, she wouldn't have dreamed of saying so, of throwing Evie's good intentions back in her face.

'Look—' She consciously brightened her voice, making herself take an interest. 'There's already snow on the mountain tops.' Against a bright blue sky it was sparkling, festively pretty. 'I hope you've brought a shovel. If this cottage we're staying in gets buried in ten-foot drifts you're going to need it!'

'No worries!' There was a hint of banked-down excitement in Evie's voice. 'The forecast on the telly promised clear skies and frosts for the entire holiday period. The only hard graft, big sister, will be building the fire up. Promise!'

She'd have to take her sister's word for it. She rarely, if ever, watched the small screen herself. She'd tried to begin with, especially when Evie stayed in to watch something she said was unmissable. Unable to concentrate on the moving images, Bella had conjured up his face every time—Jake as she'd last seen him, the hard, handsome features stamped with bitterness and contempt.

'Keeping the fires burning can be your holiday job, kiddo.' She was doing her best to enter into the spirit of this unusual Christmas gift, to ignore the scaldingly angry pain that the mere thought of Jake sent through her. 'I'll cook the turkey—you did say everything was supplied?'

She didn't need to ask. Evie had been bombarding her with every last detail ever since she'd sprung the surprise the evening before. But it gave her something to say, something to give the impression that she was looking forward to the break, taking an appreciative interest.

Strangely, her sibling seemed at a loss for words right now, clearing her throat before she pointed out, 'According to the instructions, it should be just over the brow of this hill.'

'You're the driver.' And thank heavens for that. Bella knew she would never have found her way through this bleak landscape of winter-bare mountains and the network of rutted tracks without radar, yet Evie was driving her bright red Corsa as if she'd made the journey a thousand times before.

Sure enough, as they crested the brow the cup-shaped valley below cradled a slate-roofed stone cottage backed by a windscreen of spruce, bounded on three sides by a narrow mountain stream. In the summer it would be idyllic, a popular holiday let for people who valued solitude and simple pleasures. But in the heart of the winter?

Bella suppressed a shudder and turned on a smile. Little Evie, bless her, had done this for all the best reasons. She wasn't to know that nothing, but nothing on God's earth could stop her remembering that tomorrow would be her fourth wedding anniversary— and the day after that a whole empty, hateful year since she'd finally conceded her marriage was over.

She'd tried; heaven knew she'd tried to purge him and their ill-destined marriage from her mind, but had dismally failed. He had a way of sneaking inside her head when she was least expecting it. She hated it when that happened; it made her feel she had no control over her thoughts.

'Looks cosy,' she remarked, falsely bright, trying not to notice the sudden rush of agony to her heart. The little car bounced to a halt beside the narrow wooden footbridge that spanned the stream a few yards from the cottage. Small-paned windows were built into stout stone walls, and there was a door that looked solid enough to withstand a hurricane. Bella undid her seat belt and twisted round, reaching into the back for the two canvas bags, quickly packed last night.

'We won't need much,' Evie had stated. 'Jeans and sweaters and lots of woolly socks.'

Bella had both bags out and was shivering in the icy wind, but Evie looked glued to the drivers' seat, her voice high and thin as she smacked a fist against her forehead theatrically and wailed, 'Oh, I'm such a fool! You're not going to believe this!'

'You forgot the key,' Bella sighed, resigned to footing the bill for whatever damage they did while breaking and entering. Despite her expensive secretarial training, and her recent promotion to a high-profile job, Evie's brain sometimes took on decidedly bird-like qualities.

'Nope.' She threw the key and Bella fumbled to catch it with frozen fingers. 'The milk, eggs, fresh veggies. And the turkey, would you believe? The non-perishables are here already, but I was supposed to collect the fresh stuff from the farm we passed back there.' She restarted the engine, adding, 'I clean forgot. Go on in, there's a love. Get a fire going, huh?'

Bella shrugged, flexing her stiff body, pushing her long black hair away from her face with the back of a gloved hand. It seemed sensible, but... 'How long will you be?' She hadn't noticed any sign of human habitation for what seemed like ages, and the weather forecasters had got it wrong again. Suddenly the sky was heavy with cloud, pressing against the mountain flanks, the short winter day drawing to a premature close.

'Half an hour?' Evie was releasing the handbrake. 'Get inside before you freeze.' And she was gone, circling the car on the sweep of short winter grass, narrowly missing the sturdy wooden picnic table that wouldn't see any use until families came here in the warm summer weather.

Bella smiled wryly, watching the little red car disappear over the brow of the hill. Trust Evie to forget the perishables, drive right past the place where she was supposed to pick them up! At twenty-five, three years younger than Bella, and holding down a responsible job, Evie still hadn't outgrown her occasional periods of scattiness, or the impulsiveness that was such an endearing part of her nature.

Bella shivered, glancing worriedly up at the sky. Snow was beginning to fall, shrouding the tops of the mountains. But if Evie had said she'd be back in half an hour then the farm couldn't be far away. Funny— she'd seen no sign of one herself...

Jake Fox pulled the hired Range Rover to the side of the track and consulted Kitty's scrawled instructions. For a schoolteacher his kid sister had appalling handwriting. And an unfortunate taste in men-friends if the current cry for help was anything to go on.

His brows drew together, making a forbidding, dark line above the bridge of his thin, arrogant nose. The UK was the last place he wanted to be over the festive season. He didn't need reminders of the events of a year ago.

He was in the middle of a series of successful business meetings in Geneva and had intended to fly out to Sydney, book into a hotel and settle down to paperwork, readying himself for the raft of meetings scheduled for the New Year. No stranger to concentrated work, he now embraced it with what he himself could recognise as something amounting to obsession.

He thrust the underlying reasons for that out of his head, his frown deepening as he scanned the suddenly darkening sky, the thick, suspiciously storm-like shrouds hiding the tops of the mountains. If it hadn't been for Kitty's stricken desire for his time and attention he would have been heading for the sun...

But he'd been looking out for his sister ever since his father had brought the family to ruin, his addiction to gambling on the stockmarket losing them everything—the family-run business, the four-bedroomed house in the prosperous suburbs, the lot.

Even though Kitty was now twenty-six years old he still thought of her as the wild and troubled twelve-year-old he had held in his arms and tried to comfort when their father had taken his own life. Eight years her senior, he'd felt his responsibility keenly—especially when their mother, worn out with grief and worry, had succumbed to pneumonia six months after the shock of the death of her adored husband.

He'd never thought of himself as having a protec-

tive streak, he thought wryly. But perhaps he did, to
have agreed to cancel flights, hotel rooms and drop
everything when she'd put that call through to
Geneva, catching him at his hotel before he left for
one of his most important meetings.

'I need you, Jake. Spend Christmas with me? I've
got to have someone to talk to; there's no one else I
can turn to! And, yes, before you ask, it's Harry.'

The panic in her voice caught his attention. He said
heavily, 'I thought you and he were settled.' Of all
the men Kitty had dated—and to his knowledge they
came and went like the flowers in springtime—Harry
had become a permanent fixture.

Jake liked Harry, and had guardedly learned to trust
him. Steady, good-humoured, also a member of the
teaching profession, his influence on Jake's volatile
sister had been gratifying. They'd set up home together two months ago. Kitty's letters and phone calls
had been full of joy, and he'd planned to pay off the
mortgage on their roomy Victorian house as soon as
the banns were called.

'What went wrong?' he asked.

'I can't talk about it over the phone. But it's trouble
with a capital T.' Her normally bubbly tones were
absent; she sounded at the end of her tether. 'Look, a
couple I know offered me the use of their holiday
home in Wales. I need to get away and think, and talk
everything over with you. Please say you'll come,
Jake, just for a day or two? Please?'

He mentally jettisoned his plans for a quiet working
holiday in the sun. The thought of a cottage in the
Principality, in the dead of winter, wasn't going to

make him expire from over-excitement, but it was far enough away from London. He rarely made more than flying visits to head office now. Since he had sold the Docklands apartment.

So Wales it would be, and at least he could do his best to sort out Kitty's problems—something he seemed to remember having to do all through her teens and early twenties.

And she was saying, taking his silence for tacit consent, 'I knew you wouldn't let me down, bruv. Look, I'll post directions through to your London office. Drive up on the twenty-third. I'll try and make sure I'm there ahead of you, but, in case I'm not, there's a spare key in the woodshed at the back.'

And now, the final details of her written instructions committed to memory, he restarted the engine and drove on.

The whole package must have cost Evie a small fortune, Bella decided at the end of her tour of inspection. Two bedrooms were tucked under the eaves, small but cosy, with flowery wallpaper and high brass beds spread with top-of-the-range down duvets and patchwork covers. There was a sparklingly clean bathroom and farmhouse kitchen—pine and copper, with colourful rag rugs—complete with a real Christmas tree in a tub and a box of baubles waiting to be hung. The large living room was furnished with antique pine plus squashy chairs and a huge inglenook fireplace that promised long, cosy, relaxing evenings...

And, thinking of fires, it was time she got moving. It was the least she could do to have the place warm by the time Evie got back. And the best she could do was to forget her own unhappiness and put on a festive face, she told herself toughly as she wrapped the full-length, softly padded coat around her too-slender five feet nine inches and ran across the yard to the shed to look for fuel.

Ten minutes later she was squatting back on her heels, holding out her long-fingered hands to the dancing flames curling around the tinder-dry logs in the hearth, her ears straining for the sound of an engine that would let her know Evie was back.

She'd been gone over an hour now. A good half an hour longer than she'd predicted. Standing up, Bella switched off one of the table lamps and walked to the small-paned window, peering out into the near darkness. No need to worry. She forced her tight shoulder muscles to relax. Knowing Evie, she'd probably got into conversation with the farmer's wife, accepted a welcome cup of tea and then another, oblivious to the passing of time. But it was snowing heavily now...

It was snowing heavily now, the wipers squeaking as they cleared the windscreen. Jake gritted his teeth in a humourless grin. Kitty had said she wanted peace and quiet, time to think. Well, she'd sure as hell get it, stuck out here. And if the snow fell at this rate for a couple of hours there'd be no getting away; she'd have more time than she'd bargained for.

If it didn't stop in the next thirty minutes, he'd insist on driving her out. They could get to Abergavenny, find a hotel. He made his mind up quickly, with typical decisiveness, the deed as good as done. Then thanked his own foresight in hiring the sturdy four-wheel drive.

As the vehicle crested the brow of the hill the powerful headlights illuminated the isolated cottage. He breathed a sigh of relief. There was light shining from one of the downstairs windows. There was no sign of her car so she must have parked it at the rear. At least she'd arrived. The sense of relief told him how much he'd been worrying, wondering how she'd manage if she'd been late setting out, determined to make the rendezvous no matter what the conditions were like.

Bella saw the headlights and relaxed, smiling now. Evie.

Turning back to the fire, she fed it a couple more logs, dusted down her hands and went through to the kitchen, turning on lights and hanging up her coat on the peg behind the door.

She filled the electric kettle in readiness, taking two mugs down from the dresser. They would put the food away and discuss what to have for supper over a cup of tea. And later they'd open one of the bottles of wine that were lined up on one of the work surfaces. Really get in the festive mood—dress the tree. She owed it to Evie to do her damnedest to enjoy herself because her sister had obviously gone to a lot of trouble and expense to get this set-up organised.

She heard the clunk of the car door closing and hurried through. Evie would probably need a hand unloading. There was a smile on Bella's sultry lips as she tugged at the heavy front door. She wouldn't say 'what kept you?' or grumble about the length of time she'd been. She'd...

She froze, only her hands moving, going to cover her mouth as if to stem the cry of anguished outrage.

Jake. His tall, lithe body filled the doorframe, his broad shoulders made even hunkier by the sheepskin jacket he wore. Jake. The husband she'd parted from in a welter of anger and pain. The husband she'd never wanted to have to set eyes on ever again!

What in the name of sweet reason had brought him here? And how could she hope to forget him and all the pain and disillusionment, the shattered expectations of their marriage, when the cruellest reminder of all was standing in front of her, crucifying her with those cynical black eyes?

CHAPTER TWO

BELLA couldn't speak. The shock of seeing Jake again had paralysed her, and for a long, intense moment he too was silent. But the clenching of his hard jaw, the bitter twist of his mouth, said enough. Said it all—that she was the last person he had expected or wanted to see, that she was too contemptible to waste his breath on.

Her mouth dried and her stomach clenched sickeningly when he broke the dark, silent punishment, looked beyond her into the shadowy little hallway and called out harshly, 'Kitty!'

Clenching her hands at the sides of the soft warm leggings she'd chosen to travel in, Bella's eyes went wide. She didn't understand what was happening here, asked herself if the whole world had gone crazy, or if it was only her—or him. Then she met his accusing black stare as he switched his attention back to her.

The black glitter of his eyes was dangerous. Bella tried and signally failed to suppress a shudder. 'Where is she?' he demanded. 'If you and my sister have set this up—' He left the threat hanging on the air—heavy, implicit.

'I haven't seen your sister. Why should I?' She could answer him now, now the shock was receding, her heartbeat gradually approaching normal. 'I can't imagine why you should think Kitty might be here.'

Her water-clear grey eyes glinted coolly, but the small satisfaction of showing an aloofness she was far from feeling, evaporated like a raindrop in the heat of the sun when he remarked icily, 'Don't play games with me. I endured them when we lived together. When you walked out on our marriage I no longer had to. I don't intend to lose that freedom now.'

He strode in out of the dark, snowy evening, closing the door behind him while she flinched with pain.

She had never played games with him. Never. Not in the way he obviously meant. She had never told him lies. And it was he who had first walked out, not she. And although, as he'd stated, his freedom from their relationship was a relief, he was turning the tables, heaping all the blame for what had happened on her head. Did he actually enjoy hurting her? Couldn't he see that part of the blame was his? That he had driven her to do what she had done?

For a brief, poignantly remembered time he had given her joy. Now he only gave her pain.

Her mouth trembled and her eyes brimmed with tears, turning them to shimmering, transparent silver. Barely giving her white features a glance, Jake strode into the living room, and after a moment she reluctantly followed, only to hear his steps pounding up the narrow wooden stairs that led from the kitchen to the floor above.

She'd told him Kitty wasn't here and he didn't believe her. She crossed to the brightly burning fire and wrapped her arms around her body, shivering; the combination of the chill of the hallway and the spiralling nervous tension made her whole body shake.

She could hear him opening and closing doors. For some obscure reason he thought she and his sister had set this meeting up. But why on earth should they do that? It didn't make sense. Did he think she was angling for a reconciliation—tired of earning her own living, missing his wealth, the hedonistic, self-centred lifestyle that had been hers for the taking?

Whatever, his attitude left little room for believing that he would want any part of such an obviously untenable scenario!

She pressed her fingertips to her suddenly throbbing temples. Where the heck was Evie? What on earth could be keeping her? She should have been back ages ago. With her sister around for moral support she could tell Jake where to go, where to put his nasty suspicions. Evie would back her up. They hadn't seen Kitty and didn't expect to.

Hearing him descending the stairs, she resisted the impulse to blindly run and hide and stood straighter, pulling air deep into her lungs, the midnight-jet of her long silky hair heightening her pallor.

But he didn't seem to see her as he walked straight through and out into the night, and she thought, Thank God, he's leaving! and collapsed onto a chair and clasped her hands around her knees to stop them shaking. She let the fettered tears fall freely now because he was no longer here to see her weakness.

But he was. Within minutes he was back inside, snowflakes glittering on his thick dark hair. 'There's no sign of her car. Any car. She hasn't arrived yet.' His black brows bunched with concern. 'And how did you get here?'

'On my broomstick!' His reappearance, his wit-
nessing the hateful feebleness of her tears—the shock
of seeing him here at all—made her tongue acid. But
the level look he turned on her had her muttering defensively, 'I came with Evie. She had to go back to
the farm for provisions. We're spending Christmas
here.'

A Christmas break that was meant to take her mind
off the traumatic events of a year ago—not bring her
face to face with the man who had set those events
in train, the husband who now obviously loathed and
despised her, considered himself well rid of her!

Where are you, Evie? she agonised. She felt dis-
traught, her sister's inexplicable lateness adding to her
distress. Her mind was painting pictures of the little
car stuck on an icy incline, or toppled over one of the
precipitous drops that seemed to cluster around each
and every one of the hairpin bends that made the
mountain tracks so picturesque.

She gritted her teeth. Picturesque she could do
without. She wished Evie had never had the bright
idea of arranging this holiday—and then her insides
churned around. What if Evie had invited Kitty along,
too? It was possible, given Jake's conviction she'd be
here.

She, Bella, had always got along well with Jake's
sister, but Kitty and Evie had struck up a firm friendship shortly after the wedding, where they'd met for
the first time.

Jake was convinced his sister was due here—had
she told him that much? Had he needed to get in touch
with her for some vital reason or other and couldn't,

not without coming in person, because there wasn't a phone?

Had he reluctantly driven up, swallowing his dislike of seeing his estranged wife again, because he had to talk to Kitty for some important reason?

If so, he would be desperately worried over her non-appearance, just as she was worrying over Evie. She took a deep breath and said, 'Was Kitty supposed to be joining us?'

She would have thought it highly unlikely, given that her own sister had booked this break in order to take Bella's mind off her broken marriage at this special and, for her at least, traumatic time of year. But, given his unshakable conviction, his very obvious concern...

Jake Fox dragged air deep into his lungs and exhaled it slowly, shudderingly, through gritted teeth.

She'd lost the small amount of weight she'd gained during their marriage, he noted bitterly—it had to be because of her return to her modelling career, he thought. But she was still the beautiful, sensuous woman who had drifted in and out of his dreams so maddeningly over the past twelve months. He could order his long waking hours with almost military precision, but he had found it impossible to regulate his dreams.

However, he was working on it.

He took a step towards where she was sitting, defensively hunched in an armchair that dwarfed her delicate frame, his body moving without direction from his brain.

Something about the hunted look in those crystal

eyes, the tremulous droop of the lush mouth that had been responsible for the birth of many a male fantasy, touched him despite himself.

That protective streak rearing its head again, he decided cynically.

'We need to get the facts out in the open.' Purposefully, he took the chair opposite hers. His heart was banging about under his ribcage but he'd sounded cool, in control, thank the Lord. He'd give up significantly more than his eye-teeth rather than let her know how she could still affect him and touch his heart.

He gave her a narrow-eyed stare. Her unbelievably long and heavy dark lashes had fallen, hiding her expression. The truth had always been there in her eyes if you looked long and hard enough to find it. As he'd found it—had had it forcibly thrust upon him—when he'd walked in on her and that creep, Guy Maclaine.

Abruptly he shifted his mind from that often-replayed scenario, watching her closely.

'You're here to spend a quiet Christmas with Evie, and you claim you had no idea Kitty was expected,' he stated levelly.

That was obviously what she meant him to believe. But he knew differently. Kitty, damn her, had used the ruse of needing to talk her problems over with him to get him here. She had needed peace and quiet, she'd said. Just the two of them. If her troubles had been as dire as she'd intimated she wouldn't have wanted his estranged wife and her sister around to add to the jollity!

Kitty wouldn't be turning up. That had never been her intention.

He watched Bella closely. Her confusion was very convincing. But to rise to the dizzy heights of top photographic model, internationally sought-after and universally fêted, she would have had to become a reasonably proficient actress. She could have set this whole thing up, drawing his own sister, and hers, into her web of deceit. Deceit had turned out to be her middle name.

She said nothing, merely nodded after considering his statement, the silky swathes of her hair falling forward, hiding her face.

'And I'm here because my sister begged me to be. She's in trouble, or so she said. She needed to talk and a friend had offered her the use of this place.'

The sardonic explanation of his presence brought her head jerking up, her silver eyes locking with his, clouded with more expertly portrayed confusion, her soft lips pouting with almost child-like perplexity. Over-acting, Jake decided, feeling his heart go hard— a not unusual occurrence these days. Her betrayal and subsequent defection had atrophied that particular organ.

'The three of you set this up.' A cold statement, spoken with concise deliberation. He could find no other explanation for the way he'd been tricked into coming here. 'If you'd wanted a meeting you could have made an appointment with my secretary. There was no need to go to such ridiculous lengths.'

He glanced impatiently at his watch. He had no intention of prolonging this farce. She deserved to be left here to stew, but his conscience wouldn't let him take that road.

He'd seen no sign of a phone when he'd investigated this place, so she couldn't contact anyone for transport out of here, and the way the weather was looking she could be marooned in the mountains for weeks. He'd drop her off at the first hotel they happened across on his way to Kitty's home in Chester. He'd rout his sister out of her cosy love-nest and give her the tongue-lashing of her lifetime for her part in this time-wasting piece of lunacy.

Bella pushed the hair off her face with the back of her hand. He was accusing her of conniving with their respective sisters to get him here. There could be only one reason why she would stoop to doing that—couldn't there just? To 'persuade' him to take her back.

'In your dreams!' She answered his accusation rawly. As if she would! His conceit was beyond belief!

She snapped to her feet, anger drenching through her. He had always treated her like a mindless doll, with no needs of her own, no thoughts that weren't his, without direction unless he pulled her strings. Simply a body to be seen on his arm, making him the envy of every red-blooded male around, and a gratifyingly willing body in his bed whenever he decided to remember to come home.

He wouldn't be able to believe she could exist and prosper without him. Even though he didn't want her anywhere near him, his conceit would make him believe she couldn't carry on without him and would go to any lengths to get him back.

He was on his feet, too, and the sheer breadth and

height of him swamped her, was in danger of sapping her will. But she wouldn't let his masculinity intimidate her. She would not! Drawing breath to tell him to get out of here, now, she held it, ears straining as she caught the distant sound of an engine.

'Evie!' she breathed, her eyes glowing with vindication. And not before time! She would back her up, tell this arrogant beast that any conspiracy was all in his twisted mind. Why should she want him to take her back when he was unable to give her the one thing she craved?

'Bravo!' Black eyes glinted with sardonic applause, even a hint of humour. 'Nice touch. But we both know your sister won't be showing her face within a hundred miles of this place, don't we?'

The story about Evie having popped down the road to pick up the groceries was thin, and that was putting it mildly. And Bella was still hamming it up, making a show of listening intently, so he, too, listened to the resounding silence, then snapped out an order.

'Get your things together while I rake out what's left of this fire. We're leaving. I'll drop you at a hotel.'

The faint sound of the engine had long since faded. A farmer making his way home along one of those tortuous mountain tracks, she decided tiredly. Disappointment hit her like a charging elephant. And then came the cruelly sharp anxiety. She stared at him, frowning, shaking her head.

'No. I'm staying here, waiting for Evie.' Didn't he care that something must have happened? Her happy-go-lucky, impulsive little sister had set out over two hours ago now, promising to be back within thirty minutes. Despite all his faults, he had never been a heartless man. So why wasn't he concerned?

Because he doesn't believe you, a weary little voice inside her head confirmed. He thinks the three of you set this up. She couldn't imagine why Kitty had been invited to share this break, or why she hadn't arrived yet. And she couldn't bother her head with it, not while she was so on edge, worrying herself silly over Evie's whereabouts, fighting to contain the pain of seeing him again.

She wrapped her arms around her body tightly. It was the only way to hold herself together. 'I'm staying. You go. Just get out of here.'

Stress made her voice tight and thin. He wasn't going to help find Evie, that was obvious. He didn't believe there was a thing to worry about, and was, as usual, too sure of himself and his opinions to be persuaded otherwise. But when he'd gone then maybe, with the trauma of actually seeing him again behind her, she could think of what to do.

He gave her a long, considering look, his jaw tight. Then shrugged the beginnings of misgivings away. They'd probably made adequate contingency plans. None of them were fools. Despite their plotting they must have allowed for the possibility of his abrupt removal from the set-up.

Without any doubt she'd have a mobile phone tucked away in her luggage, hidden amongst the filmy folds of the seductive nightwear she favoured, and as soon as he left she'd be using it to summon one or other of the girls to fetch her out of here.

Her pride wouldn't let her go with him, and he could understand that. Leaving with him would be tantamount to confessing that the star role in this farcical conspiracy was hers.

Bella watched him stride to the door, then sprang after him urgently, catching him up as he was tugging the outer door open.

'Phone the local police.' She couldn't use his name. 'The first call box or house you come across. Let them know she's missing. Promise!'

His heart missed a beat then thundered heavily on. He turned to her with warning reluctance, and for the first time he allowed himself to scan the face that had so relentlessly haunted his dreams over the past year. The lovely lines were taut with strain, the perfect skin white and transparent, terror lurking deep in those spellbinding eyes.

And for the first time very real misgivings flooded icily through him as he met his own fallibility. She'd been telling the truth—as she saw it. She wouldn't involve the police, set an area search in motion simply to save her pride. And if she had a mobile she wouldn't be asking him to do the phoning.

'Tell them I'll be here. I'll wait.' Her voice was ragged.

'OK,' he said roughly. He turned, then looked back at her. 'I'll contact them. And I'll be back.'

He saw her sag with relief, tears starting in her eyes, and resisted the violent urge to take her in his arms, hold her for a moment and comfort her. He walked quickly into the darkness, his throat tight, dragging his mind away from her.

Thank God it had at least stopped snowing. Even so, there was a good inch of the treacherous stuff underfoot. Swinging into the Range Rover, he reached for the key he'd left in the ignition then put both hands on the wheel, thinking hard.

The events of the last few minutes told him that Bella was desperately worried over her sister's non-appearance, that her story was true. She really believed that something dreadful must have happened. The shock of discovering that had driven Kitty's involvement out of his head, while anxiety over Evie's fate had never allowed it to enter Bella's.

In all probability they were both the innocent victims of a cruel conspiracy. He'd get to the nearest phone and contact Kitty before he involved the police. If his gut feeling was right, there would be no need.

There was a torch on the passenger seat and he used it to have a look at the time. A few minutes after six. Too early for Kitty and Harry to have gone out for the evening. Too late for her to be shopping. He should catch her at home.

He turned the key in the ignition and nothing happened.

Bella knew she had to pull herself together. Somehow. She moved briskly round the lamplit room, tweaking curtains, plumping up cushions that didn't need the attention, hoping the futile activities would settle her mind. A mind that was seething with all that was going on.

The shock of seeing Jake, here of all places. His cynical accusations. His cold admission that her absence from his life was a relief. Add Evie's disappearance to that little lot and you got a brain that was on the brink of blowing.

Sucking in her breath, she flew to the dying fire and carefully placed a few small logs on the embers. If Evie came back the poor love would be cold— She caught the thought, altered it savagely. Not if—when.

The police would soon be out looking for her, and that was an enormous consolation. She was scatty enough to have run out of petrol. Nothing more disastrous than that. And Jake had promised to come back and report, to wait with her.

The thought was deeply comforting. Yet she didn't want it to be! She wanted him out of her mind. It was the only way.

She turned from the replenished fire, satisfied that the fresh logs were beginning to flame, and Jake walked back in, his face black with temper.

As before, they faced each other wordlessly, until Bella found her voice and whispered, 'Did you find a phone?'

He couldn't have had time, surely? He'd only walked out a matter of minutes ago. She put a hand to her heart as if to still the suddenly violent pounding. Something was wrong. Terribly wrong.

He looked as if he wanted to shake her to within an inch of her life. His black eyes were ferocious, his jaw clenched, dark with the perpetual five o'clock shadow she had sometimes teased him about in former, happier, long-gone times, knowing he had to shave twice a day if he wasn't to look like a hooligan with piratical tendencies.

'Hardly.' His voice was dry. Coming further into the room, he removed his coat, tossed it over the back of one chair and sprawled down in the other. The hard line of his mouth told her he was controlling his temper, but only just; her head was beginning to ache, and there was an insistent thrumming noise inside her ears.

Both hands flew up to either side of her head, as if to hold it on her shoulders, as she rasped out thinly, 'What are you doing?'

Sprawled out in a chair while Evie was missing somewhere on the bleak, cold mountainside! Oh, how could he? Long legs in soft dark cords stretched out endlessly, only the tense, hard line of the hunky shoulders beneath the Aran sweater testifying that his pose wasn't as relaxed as he was trying to pretend it was.

'You tell me,' he came back, talking through his teeth. 'I'm in your hands. You win, for the moment.' He gave her a thin, completely humourless smile. 'Remove the distributor cap, take the rotor arm and no one's going anywhere. Evie's final chore before she high-tailed it back to civilisation? Neat. But not neat enough. I'm walking out of here at first light. You can do what you damn well like!'

den, swamping embarrassment at having
into this situation was intense.

He said nothing. Just stared at her
her thoughts, putting everything in
that would help her cope.

'They've been friends eve
you know that, of course. T
idea of getting us back
an acknowledgement
hope. 'Kitty was to
other, while my
dumped me.
around until
car.'

She
didn'
he

would need to develop a ___ ___
imagine him feeling foolish. Or used. He was always
very much in control. Of everything.

She glanced up at him, but his features told her
nothing. Blank. So what was new? Hadn't he always
closed her out, guarding his emotions, keeping them
to himself? Except when they'd been making love,
she recalled unwillingly, feeling the colour come and
go on her face. 'I'm sorry,' she whispered, her voice
thick.

She didn't know why she was apologising. His sister was just as much to blame as hers. She heaved
another log onto the fire, for something to do with her
hands. She didn't know where to put herself; the sud-

been forced

Bella verbalised

order, hoping that

since we married. But

hey obviously hatched the

together.' She smiled thinly,

f the vain futility of that forlorn

get you here, on some pretext or

devious sister drove me down and

would have been Evie who hung

she knew you'd arrived, then spiked your

saw one dark brow slowly rise at that, but

grasp the significance—not then. She moved,

ading for the kitchen. 'I'll make tea. But I warn

you, there won't be any milk.' She was trying to be adult about this—this dreadful situation. They were in it together whether they liked it or not, until the morning anyway, and there was no point in behaving like a pair of squabbling children, sulking and not speaking to each other.

'Try the fridge,' he offered drily. He'd followed her through. She wished he hadn't. It was easier to act normally if there was space between them.

Bella plugged in the kettle she'd filled earlier. It felt more like a hundred years than a couple of hours ago since she'd heard the car arrive and had confidently expected Evie to come in out of the cold, needing a hot cup of tea.

She shook her head slightly at his suggestion, even

managing a small, condescending smile. There would be no fresh provisions; she already knew that. But she crossed to the fridge and opened it, simply to humour him.

No one could have crammed another item in, even with a shoehorn. Her wretched sister's doing! She'd been nothing if not thorough! She'd been out all day yesterday—Christmas shopping, she'd said. When in reality she must have come up here, stocked the fridge, made sure everything was ready.

'I can't believe it,' she said thinly.

Jake standing beside her now, murmured, 'No?'

Bella closed her eyes. Her head spun as the warm, intimate male scent of him overpowered her, forcing her to remember how it had once been for them: the deep, endlessly intense need, the hopes, the dreams, the loving—oh, the loving...

'Aren't you going to read it?'

The laid-back taunt made her eyes flip open, erotic memories thankfully slipping away, extinguished by his obvious and habitual disbelief in her which released her to enquire breathlessly, 'Read what?'

'Oh, come on, honey!' He reached for the stainless steel handle and reopened the door.

Bella bit her lip. Why dredge up that old endearment? Why employ that tone—half-amused, half-exasperated? The tone he'd used when he'd continually brushed aside every last argument she'd ever produced whenever she'd tried to make him see things her way.

'This is the next step in the game, I imagine.' He indicated a rolled up piece of paper tied to a leg of the fresh turkey with a festive bow of scarlet ribbon. He removed it, closed the door with his foot and handed her the paper, his eyes coldly mocking. 'Your cue to straighten things out, I guess. Exonerate yourself and put me in the picture—just in case I've lost the wits I was born with and am still staring into space, wondering why you're here and Kitty isn't.'

She dropped the paper as if it were contaminated. She was going to scream, have hysterics—she knew she was; she could feel the pressure building up inside her!

Turkey legs tied up with red ribbon! Cryptic notes he seemed to know all about! His attitude—oh, his attitude! Pitying yet contemptuous...

The paper was back in her hand almost before she knew it, his steely fingers closing over her own. 'Read it,' he demanded, his voice hard, intolerant of argument.

Hand on hand, fingers on fingers. The slight contact immediately became the core of her very existence. Every atom of her body, every beat of her pulse, was centred on his touch, the abrasive warmth of his skin, the underlying steel of sinew and bone.

A whole year, and nothing had changed—not for her. She only had to look at him to need him, and his touch—ah, his touch...

Her breath quivered in her lungs, fighting against the sudden, biting constriction of throat muscles, and his hand moved abruptly away, leaving her cold with a creeping coldness that invaded every part of her.

'Well?' he prompted cuttingly. 'Don't you want to

know what it says? Or perhaps you already know? Dictated it, did you?'

Her eyes moved to his, locking with the black, glittering depths until she could no longer stand the pain. A deep shudder raked through her, and her fingers were shaking as she unfurled the note.

Despite everything, he still believed she was the prime mover, that she'd set this thing up. Well, he would, wouldn't he? When had he ever believed a word she said?

It was the final straw, she thought, her eyes blurring as Evie's distinctive scrawl danced around on the paper. Her hands flew to her face, hiding the scalding outpouring of silent, unstoppable tears, the paper fluttering to the floor again. And through the storm of her emotions she heard Jake move, heard him drawl, reading aloud, every word a bitter punishment.

'You'll forgive us eventually, I promise! But it's all your own faults. Yes, really! You won't see each other, talk to each other, even though you're still crazy about each other. Yes, you are! So marooning you together was the only answer. We were driven to it! So work things out, for pity's sake. Happy Christmas! E.'

And then silence. A long, hateful silence while the sobs built up inside her, threatening to pull her to shreds. How could Evie have done this to her? Dumped her in this hatefully embarrassing, hurtful situation?

They'd always been so close, looked out for each

other since they were children—and now this, this shattering betrayal. Oh, how could she?

She'd accepted that something like this must have happened, but she hadn't taken it in—not properly. Not until now.

The sheer awfulness of the situation hit her—Jake plainly believing she'd masterminded the entire thing, the gut-wrenching pain of seeing him, feeling his contempt, the deep anxiety she'd gone through when her sister hadn't returned, her imagination working overtime, dreaming up worst-case scenarios!

Reaction set in, releasing a crescendo of weeping, her whole body shaking with the force of it. Then the shock of feeling his hands on her shoulders, turning her gently to face him, made it worse. So much worse.

She would die if he offered her the comfort of his arms, and she'd die if he didn't!

He didn't.

He wanted to hold her, but he didn't. Hell, if he took her in his arms he'd be a lost man! Common sense, the self-discipline of a rational human being, the primary human urge towards self-protection—all down the drain.

His hands dropped to his sides. 'Calm down. You'll make yourself ill.'

His shoulders rigid, he turned to make that forgotten pot of tea. Her sobs were a little less frenzied now, he noted. The Bella he had known had never cried. She'd had, in his experience, a pragmatic approach to problems. Yet she was clearly distressed now—deeply distressed—and all he could do was offer her tea?

She was distressed because he'd seen through the charade, because he'd realised she had to be the instigator, he reminded himself cynically. Had she really imagined he wouldn't. The whole thing smacked of complicity.

Pouring tea, he recalled how she'd drawn his attention to the distant sound of an engine. He hadn't caught it himself, but she'd obviously been waiting, ears straining, for the sound that would tell her the job had been done, and that Evie was triumphantly driving out of this winter wilderness with the rotor arm in her pocket.

She hadn't been able to hide her pleasure so she'd dressed it up as relief at the return of her so-called missing sister. And then, and only then, had she thrown herself into the anxiety act, begging him to contact the police, safe in the knowledge that he wouldn't be going anywhere.

Not tonight, at least. Tomorrow he'd be out of here, even if he walked the soles clean off his shoes! Although she'd said she'd go with him, he recognised that as sheer bravado. She could stay here and play the reconciliation scene to an empty house!

He turned, put two cups of tea on the central table. She was standing where he'd left her. Not weeping now, not doing anything. Her ashen face and the anguished twist of her mouth wrenched at his guts.

His mouth went dry, his throat muscles clenching. Had she wanted a reconciliation that badly? Badly enough to make her dream up this last-ditch farce?

Not allowing himself to even think of that, he said tersely, 'Drink this; you look as if you need it.' He went to the work surface where the bottles were lined up like an invitation to a week-long bacchanalia. He selected a brandy, noting the expense she had been prepared to go to, and poured two generous measures into glasses that he unearthed from one of the cupboards.

Bella watched him from heavy eyes. The hard, lean body was full of grace, despite all that sharply honed power. She knew that body as well as she knew her own. Better. She had never tired of watching him, of drowning in the effect he had on her—an effect that was threatening to swamp her all over again with its full and shattering force.

Her stomach twisted with unwanted excitement, her pulses going into overdrive, blood throbbing thickly through her veins. She whimpered, angry with herself, with the wretched body that couldn't accept that their marriage, their love—everything—was over.

She wanted to walk out of this room but couldn't move. There was potent chemistry here, keeping her immobile, a subtle kind of magic holding her against her will. She watched him turn. He was holding what looked like two huge doses of brandy in his elegant, capable hands.

'Sit,' he commanded tersely. 'Tea and then a shot of brandy could help.'

'I don't want it.' She dragged her eyes from the heart-stopping wonder of him, fixing them on the floor, not caring if she looked and sounded like a sulky child.

She was no longer his wife, not in any real sense,

so she didn't have to let him pull her strings, tell her what to do and when to do it. Not any more.

Besottedly in love with him, she'd never made a fuss when things hadn't worked out the way she wanted them to. She'd taken it for granted that, because he loved her, the decisions he made regarding the present and the future were the best for them. She'd believed he had some grand plan, the details of which had been a mystery to her.

Love had made her turn herself into a doormat. She now knew he had never loved her—couldn't have done—so was it any wonder he'd thought nothing at all of walking all over her?

Thrusting the disturbing revelation aside, she lifted her head and gave him a defiant look. 'I'm going to bed. I've had as much of today as I can stomach.' She was doing the dictating now, and in some perverse way was almost enjoying it. 'You said you'd be making tracks in the morning. Don't go without me.' She stared at him from glass-clear, challenging eyes. 'My sense of direction is nil, as you might remember. So take it as self-preservation on my part, not a warped desire for your company.'

Let him chew that over! Engineered this unlikely set-up, had she? Conceited brute!

She was at the foot of the wooden staircase when his terse voice stopped her in her tracks.

'Have you eaten today? You won't get far on what will probably turn out to be a ten-mile hike to get to anything remotely approaching civilisation on a diet of vinegary spleen.' His tone wasn't remotely humorous, nor even a touch compassionate. It was totally judgemental. 'Was losing weight part of your job requirements? Stick insects still high fashion, are they?'

She ignored the lash of anger in his voice. What did he care, anyway? She could get thin enough to disappear with the bathwater and he wouldn't blink an eye. It would save him the trouble of divorcing her.

But he was right about one thing—she should at least try to eat something. The walk out of here tomorrow would be exhausting, and the single slice of toast she'd had at breakfast was nothing more than a distant memory.

Much as she now hated to do anything he suggested—a backlash from the days when she'd practically turned herself inside out to please him—she turned back, and would have rooted around for the bread and some cheese and taken it through to eat by the probably dying fire, but he got in before her.

'I'll fix something. There appears to be enough food laid on to provision a garrison so it shouldn't be difficult. Why don't you drink that tea?'

No anger now, merely a smooth, impersonal politeness. It reminded her of her former attempts to be adult about the situation. So she'd play it his way—forget being bolshie, drink her tea like the man said.

It was tepid, but she got through half of it and ignored the brandy. He was sipping his as he moved around. Her eyes narrowed as she watched him. He was good in a kitchen, and she'd never known it.

She'd always been there, waiting for him to fit in a visit home between his tight work schedules. So pleased to see him, so eager for the time he could spare her—had condescended to spare her!—that she'd practically fallen over herself to make their time together as smoothly memorable as possible. After all, she'd had little else to do until she'd taken the initiative and gone back to work. He'd hated that!

The helping of grilled Cumberland sausages and tomato halves he quickly and efficiently produced was enormous enough to make her groan inwardly, and the mug of milky cocoa made her eyes go wide.

Had he secretly yearned for nursery food while she'd dished up sophisticated delicacies—potted shrimps, *navarin* of lamb, home-made sorbets so delicious they brought tears to the eye? All exquisitely served on the finest bone china—accompanied by superb wines, of course.

All the effort and dedicated planning that had gone into every meal she had ever produced for him, when all the time he might well have preferred a plate of sausages and a mug of cocoa!

Now she would never know. She most certainly wouldn't ask.

The forced intimacy of the situation frayed her nerve-endings, while the heart-clenching nearness of him on the opposite side of the small table brought the sensations she'd been battling to forget for a whole year burgeoning back to life. Which didn't help her appetite.

And she couldn't make an attempt at light, relaxing conversation. Relaxation didn't get a look in while he was around. And they didn't have a single thing to say to each other that didn't reek of contention.

Even the small sound of cutlery on earthenware

platters became too much to bear. She stood up, pushing back her chair more sharply and clumsily than she'd intended.

'Thank you.' She meant for the food she had barely touched, the cocoa she hadn't touched at all. 'But I think I'll turn in. One way or another, it's been an extremely unpleasant day.'

She made it to the stairs before he had time to respond. She truly hadn't meant to snap, but hadn't been able to keep the acid out of her voice.

Her hair prickling on the back of her neck, she bounded up the staircase. She felt like a rabbit with a fox on its heels. Jacob Charles Fox by name, and foxy by nature, she thought half-hysterically as she breathlessly gained the room she'd earmarked for herself long hours ago when she'd innocently believed she'd be sharing the isolated cottage with Evie.

But he didn't follow her, as she feared he might, to drag her down and force her to eat the food he'd cooked. Of course he didn't.

Why the heck should he want to bother? she reminded herself tiredly as she sagged back against the door, one hand at her breast as if to still the wild beating of her heart. Secure in her room, with no sound of following footsteps or angry commands from below, she couldn't imagine why she'd panicked.

He had done what he would have considered to be his duty. Reminded her that she had to eat, produced the food. It was up to her whether she ate it or not. He couldn't care either way. So the absence of a lock on the door was no problem either, was it? He wouldn't try to claim his conjugal rights.

He didn't want his rights. He couldn't care less.

Jake heard her thumping up the stairs, his mouth quirking with a reluctant smile. Her languid grace had always been part of her fabled mystique, and now she was clumping around like an ill-disciplined hoyden in hobnailed boots. She who had always been so poised, so amiably cooperative, had developed a will of her own—if his hijacking was anything to go on—not to mention a sharp little tongue.

She must have been desperate to try and work things out between them to have pulled a stunt like this.

He still didn't want to think about the ramifications, but knew he had to. And, let's face it, he hadn't made it easy for her to approach him in a more conventional manner—out of the country far more than he was in it, deliberately avoiding her and anyone who knew her.

He finished the remains of his brandy and leaned back in the chair, long fingers toying with the stem of the glass, his mind absorbed.

Over the past year he'd avoided all contact and allowed her none. His solicitor had paid her allowance into her bank account each month, and those of his staff who knew his movements had been instructed to be politely noncommittal if his estranged wife had ever shown any desire to know his whereabouts.

As far as he knew, she never had. It had appeared that she, too, had written their three years of marriage off as experience—one, in his case, never to be repeated—and was getting on with her life, with the resumption both of her modelling career and her steamy, hole-and-corner affair with the much-married Maclaine.

His mouth tightened. He could never forgive that ugly betrayal, her cold-blooded deceit. Never!

He pushed the empty glass across the table, picked up her untouched one, swallowed the contents in one long draught and snapped to his feet.

However long and loudly she protested he couldn't believe she was an innocent victim of sibling mischief. For one thing, his sister knew better than to take it into her head to meddle with his life. She knew he refused to have Bella's name mentioned in his presence.

He was sure Bella had set the whole thing up, somehow convincing Kitty that deceiving him into coming here was in his best interests. Not too difficult a task to accomplish, given the way she'd pulled the wool over his eyes through three years of marriage!

Well, she'd wanted him here and now she'd got him here, so they might as well have things out in the open. And whatever her reasons, and however desperate those reasons were, he had one answer only.

There was no going back. It was over. If she had any doubts at all it was time they were knocked on the head. And there was no time like the present...

He squared his shoulders and strode to the stairs.

CHAPTER FOUR

BELLA was too strung up to sleep. In any case, it was hours before her normal bedtime. The paperback she'd brought along to read wasn't making any sense. The words slid past her eyes. She was taking nothing in. She closed the book and shivered.

The room was cold, and to make matters worse she'd discovered that Evie—rot her socks!—had performed yet another major interfering act. Her devious little sister must have sneaked into her room at home while Bella had been in the shower and replaced the old, cosy pyjamas she'd packed herself with slivers of sheer silk and lace—the sort of seductive nonsense she hadn't worn since she and Jake had been living together.

Her first defiant thought had been to go to bed in the leggings and woolly sweater she was wearing. Every last thing she'd bundled into the canvas bag the previous evening had been replaced.

No serviceable jeans and cosy sweaters to be found, just fabulous designer gear, almost forgotten leftovers from her time as Jake's wife. They had been languishing, unworn, at the back of a cupboard at the flat she shared with that devious, double-dealing sister of hers!

She couldn't trek out of here, heading for

Aberwhatever-it-was, wearing a long slinky shirt or flowing silk trousers!

Nearly spitting with rage she'd stripped off the comfy leggings and sweater, reserving them for the morning, and hugged into a clinging dream of white satin-sheen silk, the tantalisingly revealing lace top supported by the narrowest, flimsiest of shoestring threads.

What had those two she-devils had in mind? A flaunting, a seduction, a reconciliation followed by Happy-Ever-After? What did they have between their ears? Fluff, or rocks?

Her eyes savage with bottled-up temper, she dug her head into the pillow and dragged the duvet up over her ears to shut out the sound of the howling wind. And heard instead the squeak of the door hinges, followed one second later by Jake's incisive voice.

'It's time we talked.'

'Get out of here!'

Bella shot up against the pillows, regardless of the next-to-nothing she was wearing, her eyes narrowed with temper. She had never been this angry in the whole of her life, and now she had someone to vent it on!

Her formative years had been spent in a restless round of moving from one place to another, the family being dragged by her feckless father to wherever the grass was supposedly greener but never was. She'd become adept at keeping her head down, quiet as a mouse, in case she got noticed and hauled into her parents' blistering, roof-raising rows.

Then there had been marriage to the man who could have given her everything but hadn't. And the only legacy she had from their marriage was bitterness.

She had tried to be everything he wanted her to be: glamorous, cool, acquiescent, the perfect wife, anxious—too anxious—to hold onto a will-o'-the-wisp, workaholic husband who was here today and gone tomorrow.

Here today and gone for at least a month! she amended in her head. Well, the black-eyed devil had finally walked out for good, and now she didn't have to subordinate herself to him or anyone else!

'I said, get out,' she repeated when he made no move.

He was seemingly rooted to the spot in the open doorway, his straddle-legged stance familiarly dominant, thumbs hooked into the back pockets of his jeans, dark hair falling over one eye, the unintentional designer stubble adding to the aura of rakish danger that was coming off him in waves, filling the room...

Tantrums suited her, he thought, hooded eyes appraising the wild black tumble of hair falling over naked creamy shoulders, the hectic flares of colour on those perfect cheekbones, the silver fire of her eyes, the tempting glimpse of pert, palm-sized breasts glimmering beneath the lace of that piece of seductive night wear he remembered so well. One out of many such pieces of sorcery, designed to send a man out of his mind...

He hauled his unwise thought processes back on line. Sure, she could still fire him up, but it was only common or garden lust, not the rare and precious bloom of love. That had died when he'd moved heaven and earth to get back to her for what had been left of their third wedding anniversary—and found her wrapped around Maclaine.

Bleak anger settled in his heart, turning it to stone. Had Maclaine dumped her? Was that what this was all about? Had she set this thing up—wasting his time, trying his patience to the limit—because she was conceited enough or stupid enough to believe that she only had to bat those fabulous lashes at him to get him to take her back, live with her and miraculously forget she was an adulterous bitch?

Sure, she'd told him in no uncertain manner to get out of her room. But that was only for openers; the end game would be something else entirely.

She'd made no attempt to cover herself—and what sensible woman packed such man-trap bait for a holiday in the winter wilds of Wales with her kid sister?

Her protestations of innocence regarding her part in this wearisome farce would have held a darn sight more water if she'd been muffled in flannelette right up to her pretty pink ears!

'Right.' He cleared his throat. He tried to pull his eyes from her but couldn't; they were stubbornly intent on drinking in all that sensual loveliness, and there didn't seem to be a damn thing he could do about it. 'Let's get things sorted out.'

His voice had husky undertones, Bella noted. Oh, he'd tried to make it crisp, but he'd dismally failed. She knew that tone, recognised the sultry gleam in those hooded eyes. He wanted her. He couldn't disguise it. Not from her.

Two years into their marriage, around the time she'd gone back to work with Guy, he'd stopped wanting her. He'd barely been at home at all, and had been exhausted when he was. The lust that had led him to marry her had finally been slaked. But it hadn't completely died...

The shock of it made her stomach twist, ignite with curling flames of fever that rampaged through her body. She sucked in a sharp breath and dragged the duvet up to her chin. The passion of her rage with Evie and Kitty for landing her in this mess had encompassed him, making her oblivious to what she was wearing.

'Go away.' She knew she sounded feeble now, hated herself for it. And, far from doing as she'd said, he took a few more paces into the room. Any closer and she'd weakly give in to the temptation to beg him to take her in his arms, hold her and make love to her again. Beg him to take them both back to the beginning, when she'd believed everything to be perfect and that he could give her everything she wanted.

'I'll go when you've explained why you were so desperate to get me here.'

The delayed modesty, the wide, troubled eyes, didn't fool him. It was all a cynical act. It took one to know one, he thought tiredly, wanting to get this sorted out, packed away and put behind him as he had assumed—wrongly, it would seem—it had been for the whole of the past twelve months.

'You don't believe a word I say,' she accused, her

voice shaky. He thought she was a scheming liar. It
hurt. It shouldn't, because she ought to be used to it,
but it did. Unbearably.

Her eyes filled with tears. If he didn't leave this
room, right now, she'd go to pieces, and her pride
wouldn't let that happen twice in one day. Just as her
pride hadn't let her try to make contact of any kind
with him after he'd ended their marriage by walking
out.

'Just tell me what it's all about,' he suggested
tiredly. Suddenly he felt drained. He didn't want to
argue with her, to have to play it her way and coax
and cajole her into explaining herself. He wanted out.

Bella saw bored indifference, heard it in his voice,
and anger stirred again, deep, deep inside her. 'How
can I, when I don't know?' she said through gritted
teeth. She saw him shrug, turn away, and knew she
wanted to feel relief because he was on his way out
but, perversely, didn't.

She wanted to beg him to stay, to stop accusing her
of something she hadn't done, talk to her, just talk to
her, treat her like an intelligent human being for once.

'Well, don't say I didn't give you the opportunity,'
he said tonelessly. 'I can't force you to tell me why
you set this up, and quite frankly I don't want to put
myself to that kind of trouble. If you've blown the
opportunity to tell me your reasons you've only yourself to blame.

'I'll be leaving at first light, and you won't be going
with me. Even getting to the nearest farmhouse and a
telephone won't be a picnic, and I'll make better

headway on my own. Let me know if you want me to arrange transport to get you out of here.'

Closing the door behind him, he clattered down the staircase. No way could he spend the night tossing and turning in a bed only a few feet away from hers, with only a partition wall separating them.

Seeing her again had brought needs he'd subjugated for twelve arid months bludgeoning back to life. He was only flesh and blood!

Hell! Here he was, Jake Fox, subject of enough articles in the financial press to fill a ten-ton container, having made his first paper million on the money markets before he was twenty-two and now, at thirty-four years of age, the head of his own worldwide insurance company—yet he was totally unable to handle this woman and what she did to him, take her dubious machinations in his stride.

But hadn't she always made a sucker out of him?

Tossing an armload of dry logs on the embers, he sank into a chair, almost welcoming the hypnotic howl of the wind, the insistent memories that now could not be denied...

The very first time he'd set eyes on her...

The first time he set eyes on her she was wearing a gold satin beaded shift that shimmered when she moved. And how she moved!

Clutching an unwanted, untouched glass of white wine in his hand, he couldn't find words to describe what he was seeing—the sinuous grace, the endless legs, the softly seductive curves of hip and breast. The sheer poetry as her head turned slowly on the perfection of the long and fragile stem of her neck. The strange, fabulous eyes meeting his briefly across the room, holding for a moment—almost as if the contact puzzled her—before she turned back to her companion.

He was holding his breath, he discovered. He hadn't wanted to come to this party. But he hadn't not wanted to, either—just killing time until his dinner date.

'Eyes off, buddy!' Alex muttered at his side. 'The lady's taken.'

'Sorry?' Jake's brows met. He'd bumped into Alex Griffith in the City, just as he'd emerged from his Lombard Street head office, his mind still on his recent successful Far Eastern acquisition trip.

Friends since schooldays, they kept in touch more—as now—by luck than arrangement.

'Have dinner?' Alex had suggested.

Jake had shaken his head in regret, they had a lot of catching up to do. 'Sorry. I promised to feed Kitty at The Dorchester. She's thinking of applying for a teaching post in Chester. Wants my advice.'

'Not boyfriend trouble this time?' Alex's tawny eyes had crinkled at the corners and Jake had grinned.

'Happily not, it would seem. Though I'm not counting my chickens. Something like that could be behind the sudden need to move to the sticks.'

His kid sister brought as much dedication to her social life as she did to her chosen profession. And more often than not Jake was landed with the job of picking up the pieces. Looking out for Kitty was something he'd got used to. What else were brothers for—especially as there were no parents around to sort out the crises she seemed to thrive on?

'Tomorrow? Lunch?'

'Flying out to Dubai.'

'Tell you what,' Alex had shot a glance at his watch. 'I'm due at this cocktail thrash around now. Duty thing—know how it is? Daren't miss it, or I'd suggest a quiet drink. Why not keep me company?'

So here he was, almost wishing he'd not tagged along, until his attention had been riveted by the raven-haired beauty in the shimmering dress. He couldn't take his eyes away.

'Who is she?'

'The face of La Donna.' Alex hadn't had to ask who Jake was talking about. 'Shock to the system, what? I've met her once or twice. Got myself introduced during an interval at Covent Garden. But no dice. If I thought I stood a chance I'd be in there, trying my luck—along with the rest of the male population!'

Jake ignored that, dismissed it as an irrelevance, although it was to come back and haunt him time after time. 'The face of what?' The question was spiked with urgency, a tinge of irritation.

'Where've you been the last couple of years, buddy? No, don't tell me—too busy plotting how to make your company's next billion to read the glossies or watch the hoardings!'

Then as if he sensed the brooding intensity in the dark eyes that suddenly flicked his way, Alex cut the banter and volunteered, 'Appropriately, her name's

Bella. Bella Harcourt, supermodel. She was picked to be the face of La Donna—cosmetics and stuff. Since then her career's taken off in a big way. And the guy she's with is head of the agency which handles the La Donna account. Guy Maclaine—a big name in advertising circles. He took her under his wing from the outset.'

'And?'

'And into his bed. Rumour has it he's going for his second divorce, and that the answer to every man's sexual fantasies will be Mrs Guy Maclaine the third.'

Over Jake's dead body!

His eyes narrowed, intent, Jake watched the way she smiled at Maclaine, never moving from his side, her sinuous body curving into the shelter of his like a delicate vine seeking support.

Maclaine was a big brute, with the kind of near-ugly looks some women might find attractive. She obviously did. But if he could do it, he'd take her away from him.

He had never felt like this before. The assault on his emotions, the upheaval going on in his normally rational mind, would have rocked him on his heels had he not surrendered himself to the inevitability of what was happening here.

Without false modesty he knew he was what his mother would have called 'eligible'. Neither repellent nor in his dotage, and going places in the dangerously unstable world of high finance, beautiful women came with the territory. They came and they went; he didn't have time for a committed relationship and was always careful to point that out. But this—this was something very different...

He picked his moment, shouldering his way through the knots of brightly partying people just as Maclaine was politely allowing himself to be cornered by a red-haired, red-taloned woman of questionable sobriety.

'Jake Fox,' he introduced himself, catching a flicker of uncertainty in those strangely fabulous eyes, an automatic withdrawal. 'Single, solvent, law-abiding.'

He could have added 'besotted', but didn't. And wouldn't—not until he'd come to terms with it himself, with this new and terrifyingly exciting experience. But he wasn't going to waste time on preliminaries either.

'I'm giving my sister dinner tonight; I would very much like you to join us. The Dorchester. If you need reassurance that I am neither a seducer or a white-slaver, then Alex Griffith—whom I believe you've met—can vouch for my integrity.'

He angled his shoulders, effectively screening her from the rest of the party-goers, consciously staking his claim to her undivided attention. And watched as a million glittering lights danced in her eyes, her lush mouth quirking as she tilted her head back on her long, long neck.

His heart thumped violently. If she told him to get lost he'd have to try another tack, pursue her until she gave in out of sheer exhaustion!

The smile she had been trying to swallow defeated her, and she laughed. It was a ripple of perfection amongst the babble and shriek going on around them.

'You have an intriguingly novel approach, Mr Fox! Direct, but not explicitly offensive. Tell me, does it always work?'

'I don't know. I've never tried it before.' He grinned—probably fatuously, he thought. Her voice was as beautiful as she was. 'And it's Jake. And you're gorgeous. And dinner—you will join us?'

She gave no direct answer. 'You've been watching me. Since you arrived with Alex you've been watching me.'

A simple statement of fact. Yet it made his heart lilt. Apart from that brief moment when their eyes had locked she had, to all appearances, concentrated all her attention on Maclaine. But appearances were deceptive, because she'd been aware of him, aware of the way he'd been watching her, mesmerised. Aware. Of him. Maclaine might be her lover, but that didn't mean he couldn't cut him out!

'Guilty. But, looking the way you do, you must take the blame.'

Suddenly her poise fell away. Her head drooped forward and soft tendrils of the artfully piled lustrous, midnight-dark hair gently moved against the pale, fragile neck, awakening in him a deep, atavistic desire to protect.

It was then he knew. Knew without a shadow of doubt that he wanted to possess this woman in every way there was. Take her, hold her, care for her. Make her his, and only his.

Marry her.

If marriage had ever crossed his mind it had been as something to be thought about some time in the distant future. When the future was safe, secure. When he was sure—sure that what he had to offer was solid and firm, couldn't be blown away by the cruel winds of chance that destroyed home and family in their backlash. As he had seen his home and family virtually destroyed by his father's obsessive and disastrously unsuccessful gambling on the world money markets.

But she had driven all that caution out of his head.

'You will join us.' He made it a statement, as if there could be no question about the way their relationship would begin and develop. He didn't know he'd been holding his breath until she suddenly raised her head, the brilliance of her eyes, her smile, stunning him.

'You've made me an offer I can't refuse.' Mischief silvered her eyes with dancing starlight. 'I'm dying to meet your sister!'

Then, just as quickly, her smile faded and her eyes became thoughtful, as if she was wondering what it was that had made her accept his invitation. With a minimal shrug of exquisite shoulders she turned to murmur her excuses to Maclaine, and Jake knew then—precisely then—that she was his...

Bella and Kitty had got along famously; dinner had been an unqualified success. Even if Bella had given her attention almost exclusively to the younger girl he had been content to watch and wait, knowing by the heightened colour that had glowed along her perfect cheekbones, the way she'd immediately veiled her eyes if they encountered his, that she'd been just as aware of the sizzling sexual tension as he was.

Leaving her at the mews apartment she'd shared with her younger sister, he had taken her acceptance of his offer to give her lunch the next day for granted. He'd rescheduled his Dubai meetings and had set out to win what he'd already considered his.

They'd been married eight weeks later. He had claimed the woman he'd been born to love, promising to keep her unto him until death did them part...

So much for promises, for dreams. Pain pushed at him. He pushed it away. He'd already spent too long on the rack of jealousy, so why prolong the agony? His face set, he raked out the dying embers and went slowly upstairs. Tomorrow couldn't come soon enough.

Still sleepless, Bella heard his feet on the uncarpeted stairs and stared into the darkness, wide-eyed, holding her breath.

But the footsteps passed her door, and she curled herself on her side and cried herself to sleep. Because she had wanted him to come to her, to make love to her for one last time, to give her a final memory she could live with.

The memory she did have, of the single, blistering word he'd used before turning on his heels and walking out on her and Guy, was too demeaning to live with.

CHAPTER FIVE

BELLA came awake to the distinctive aroma of freshly brewing coffee wafting up from the kitchen directly beneath her bedroom.

The window was heavily curtained, so she had no way of knowing if the late winter dawn had broken, but one thing she did know: Jake was getting ready to leave. Without her.

She wasn't going to stay here on her own!

Jumping out of bed, shivering in the chilly air, she scrambled into the warm leggings and sweater she'd worn the day before and pushed her feet into her sturdy walking shoes, panic making her heartbeat very fast.

There was no time for refinements, even the most basic ones such as bathing, or brushing her hair. She wouldn't put it past him to be walking out of here right now, creeping out, because he wouldn't want her to wake and come racing after him! He had certainly made it perfectly clear that he didn't want her tagging along, under any circumstances. He didn't want her anywhere near him.

Well, he couldn't force her to stay. So she'd dog his footsteps every inch of the way, and if he didn't like it he could lump it!

Already breathless from her haste, she flew down the stairs and arrived in the kitchen with a clatter. The room was filled with clear bright light and the enticing fragrance of coffee. Jake, wearing the bulky sweater and warm dark cords he'd had on yesterday, was staring out of the window.

'No need to break your neck. Nobody's going anywhere,' he said drily.

He turned from the window, his mouth curling. But it wasn't a smile, Bella saw. That tight-lipped grimace could easily have developed into a full-blown snarl if he'd let it; she didn't have to be an expert in facial expressions to recognise that. But it didn't stop her wretched body responding to him as if the reaction had been programmed in, right from the day of her birth.

He hadn't shaved, and the darkness of his tough jawline was more than the mere affectation of designer stubble. It made him look more dangerous, more forbiddingly exciting than ever before. And what was he talking about? Why had he altered his plans?

Answering her unspoken questions, he narrowed his eyes and drawled softly, 'You even have the weather on your side. So how did you manage that? Magic?'

He turned abruptly away, bunching his hands in the pockets of his trousers, staring bleakly through the window at the winter wasteland.

Pushing past the hurtful contempt of his words, Bella made sudden sense of what he was implying and went to stand beside him at the window, careful not to brush against him—because touching him would be her undoing, she knew darn well it would.

Stealthy snow had fallen silently in the night, blown into drifts by the howling wind. Drifts of the glittering, pure white stuff were piled up against the sturdy cottage to the height of the window-frame. Imprisoning them here together. Evie and Kitty couldn't have hoped for a better result!

'There's coffee in the pot.' He stepped back quickly, away from her. She could sense the tension in his hard body, hear it in his dark, gravelly voice.

She was right; he couldn't bear her to be anywhere near him. Finding her with Guy on that fateful night had made her physically repulsive to him. Yet there had been moments when she'd hoped...

'We're going to have to try to live with this impossible situation.'

She could hear him moving about, and she could detect resignation in his voice now. A toneless monotone that told her quite plainly that being forced to endure her undiluted company was not something he was wildly excited about.

She could have done without his earlier sarcastic implication that she'd magicked up a snowstorm to keep him here. Very much against his will. She didn't know which hurt the most, bitter sarcasm or bleak resignation, but she wasn't going to give him a clue to the way he was tearing her to pieces.

Turning reluctantly to face him, her eyes went wide. He was shrugging into his sheepskin coat, already turning up the collar against the bitter weather outside.

He was going to try his level best to get out of here, preferring to take his chances in the arctic wil-

derness out there rather than spend another moment
with her. He was leaving her stranded, walking out
on her, dismissing her from his life all over again!

She knew he didn't love her, or trust her. But she
hadn't realised just how much he hated her.

'Where are you going?' Her voice sounded tinny,
frantic even, and her face had gone red. She could
feel heat creeping all over her skin. She had sounded
like a nagging wife, but she couldn't help it. She
didn't want him walking out on her. Not again.

'Don't worry. You and the weather have me neatly
trapped.' His voice sounded as cold as the snow on
the mountain tops. 'Though what you hope to achieve
is beyond me, particularly since you refuse to be hon-
est enough to tell me.'

Bella narrowed her eyes into slits and glared right
back at him, her temper rising rapidly now. How
could you hate a person yet want him with a force
that was pretty near overwhelming? Were love and
hate really the different sides of the same coin, as
people said?

He went to the outer door and drew back the bolts.
'I'm going to dig a way through to the fuel store. I'd
appreciate it if you did your part and fixed breakfast.'

He sounded weary, Bella noted crossly. Weary of
the situation he found himself in. Weary of her. She
watched him force the door open against the weight
of snow, her chin jutting mutinously.

Anger was her only defence. She dredged up every
last bit she could find. Do as you're told; she mim-
icked his voice inside her head. And vowed she
wouldn't. Not ever again.

Besides, would it hurt him to offer her a kind word? Or, if he really couldn't manage that, simply a civil one would do! Didn't the insensitive brute remember what day it was? Christmas Eve—their fourth wedding anniversary! Did the date mean so little to him that he'd blanked it out of his mind?

Tears welled in her eyes and she blinked them furiously away, despising herself for the weakness of wanting things he could never give her—his love, his trust, the way things had been for them at the very beginning, when it had been as if he had known she was his woman, and had reached out and taken her.

And she'd gone willingly because, almost from the time they'd met, she'd known she was his—for always.

But it hadn't turned out that way. The veneer of perfection had been very thin. Scratch it, and something ugly was staring you in the face.

As soon as he was out of sight she reached for her padded coat. She hadn't wanted him to walk out on her, but she was going to walk out on him. She couldn't and wouldn't endure the situation a moment longer!

Bella knew she was acting irrationally, but how could she think straight when he was around, looking at her with those black, contemptuous eyes, making it plain he believed she had instigated this unholy mess?

Walking out of here would show him just how wrong he was about that! And remove her from the disastrously growing temptation to try to make him believe she still needed him, that she only had to see him, hear his voice, to crave the touch of his lips, his hands—because for her the wanting had never stopped.

And even if he did believe her—which was highly unlikely—his vaguely contemptuous pity would be the best she could hope to achieve. He would tell her to control her libido until she could get back to Guy. And that she could do without!

Because of the wind direction there was less snow piled up in front of the cottage than there was at the rear. The sun shone brightly from a clear blue sky, and that was a heartening omen. She'd go carefully, she promised herself, sucking in lungfuls of the cold, cold air, pick her way until she came to the nearest habitation.

She'd show him she hadn't planned this sick farce! By taking this initiative, she'd damn well prove it!

By the time he'd split enough dry logs to last for twenty-four hours, Jake's temper was high. And rising. He'd long since discarded his sheepskin coat, the heavy exercise keeping him warm, but his trousers were wet through to well above his knees—the unpleasant result of wading through the drifts to get to the shed to look for a shovel to clear the damn stuff!

He replaced the axe and shovel in the shed, flung his coat over his shoulder, gathered up an armful of logs and set off along the track he'd cleared from the shed to the cottage. He'd hoped for a rapid thaw, but it looked as if he wasn't going to get one. Great snow clouds were gathering ominously now, blocking out the sky.

He had never threatened physical harm to a woman in his life, but right now he felt like shaking Bella until her teeth fell out!

Why wouldn't the woman come clean and tell him exactly what she'd wanted to achieve when she'd ganged up with the sisters from hell and tricked him into coming here? The frustration of not knowing was almost worse than the deed itself.

There was no sign of breakfast, and the coffee-pot was cold. He told himself he wasn't surprised, and went through to dump the logs on the hearth, eyeing the cold ashes grimly.

She was probably holed up in her room, painting her nails and doing her face, expecting him to do all the donkey work!

He took the stairs two at a time, his black frown deepening as the wet fabric of his trousers clung clammily to his legs. If they were going to survive this damned incarceration without coming to blows there was going to have to be some give and take around here!

It took him less than five minutes to discover she was nowhere in the cottage, and mere seconds more to check out the front and verify what he'd sinkingly begun to suspect.

Footprints heading out of there, imprinted in the deep snow. Had the woman gone completely mad?

He collected his coat, glowered at the sky and slammed the cottage door behind him. Attention seeking, that was what this latest crazy stunt was all about!

He'd made his irritation with the situation pretty clear, refusing to play along with her game—whatever it was. So she'd trudged out into the snow, knowing full well he would feel obliged to fetch her back, thereby forcing him to give her his undivided attention.

When picking out this cottage for their 'unexpected' reunion, she'd have made good and sure it was remote, far enough from any other habitation to make getting out on foot anything but easy—and totally impossible in these conditions.

And if he didn't have a conscience he'd sit back and let her get on with it, leave her to come crawling back when she realised that playing the injured heroine wasn't getting results!

By his reckoning, he'd spent around half an hour clearing the path and splitting wood. Even if she'd shot out of the front door the moment he'd exited the back, she couldn't have gone far in that small amount of time. And when he caught up with her he'd haul her back and lay down a few firm ground rules. By hell, he would!

Half an hour later he'd followed her trail to the rim of the valley and over, zig-zagging to avoid obvious drifts and on across the flanks of the now trackless mountains. Trouble was, it had started snowing again almost as soon as he'd set out, and it was rapidly becoming a blizzard.

The powdery snow was being blown around in ever-thickening flurries, filling in the marks of her passage. If he gave the storm another ten minutes, he wouldn't have a clue how to track her down. If he didn't find her soon, he never would.

Anxiety quickened his heart rate and he forced himself to move faster, cursing the elements. Despite her height, she was too fragile to last long in these desperate conditions.

He thought of the slenderness of her bones, the delicate grace of that ultra-feminine body, and groaned, pushing himself harder. His breathing was ragged now, more from the persistently clawing anxiety than from the very real exertion.

If anything happened to her he would never forgive himself.

When a rent in the swirling clouds of snow revealed a figure up ahead, gallantly trying to get up off her knees and pathetically failing, the sense of relief he felt forced him to face what he'd tried so hard to hide—he still cared deeply for the little witch. If he'd lost her out here his life wouldn't have been worth living; his future wouldn't have been worth having.

It took him two desperate minutes to reach her, to scoop her up from her knees and hold her as tightly as he could without crushing her slender bones.

'Oh, Jake—'

Her voice was a whispery thread of sound against the wail of the wind, but he heard it, and it reached deep inside him and touched him where it hurt. It hurt like hell.

'Don't talk,' he commanded gruffly, his heart twisting inside him as his hands went to steady her shoulders to allow him to search her face.

White skin was transparent with fatigue; lips were tinged blue with cold. But her eyes were clear bright pools, pools he could drown in, and the barriers went crashing down, each and all of them, as she spoke to him.

'I'm so sorry, so sorry. Criminally...stupid...' The words were strung out, as if she hadn't the strength to say them but would, even if it was the last thing she ever did. 'Stupid thing...to do.'

'I said, don't talk,' he reiterated thickly, his throat tight. He rubbed the balls of his thumbs gently over the parchment-thin skin stretched over her cheek-bones, then cradled her head between his hands and bent to touch his lips to hers, moving them slowly, softly, transmitting what he could of his warmth to her.

He felt the sweet movement of her cold lips beneath his—opening, receptive, stroking, growing warmer, much warmer now. His heart rate quickened, sending the blood pounding thickly through his veins, until the smothered whimper of pleasure that seemed to come from the depths of her being—sapping what little energy she had left—had him reluctantly moving his mouth from hers.

This wasn't the time, and it most decidedly wasn't the place.

'Let's get you home,' he muttered, sweeping her into his arms. 'Trust me, you'll soon be warm and dry.'

'Jake—I can walk!'

'Shut up,' he ordered smoothly, briefly touching his lips to her eyelids, closing the fatigue-bruised skin over those perfect, precious eyes. Then he lengthened his stride. The elements would have to do a damn sight better than this if they wanted to stop him taking her to safety!

He barely noticed the weather as he fought through the blizzard, and her slight weight was nothing. Immeasurable relief overrode everything else; aching muscles didn't get a look in.

At one point she seemed to fall asleep, nestled in his arms, her head tucked in beneath his chin. But she woke when he shouldered open the cottage door, momentarily cuddling closer into his body before murmuring, 'Put me down, Jake. You must be exhausted.' She was deeply reluctant to leave the haven of his arms, to relinquish the closeness of the last hour when he'd found her, held her and kissed her and carried her back every step of the way. But his effort had been monumental and, strong though he was, every muscle had to be aching.

If only they could stay this close, scrub out the past and build on the future...

'I've managed this far; a few more steps won't hurt me.'

There was no condemnation in his voice, just a gruff thread of something she couldn't put a name to, and she wound her arms around his neck as he carried her up to the bathroom with no apparent effort at all.

He slid her down his body to put her on her feet, and she did her best not to sway or wobble. Out there, when the storm had worsened, she'd been truly frightened. But her hero had come and brought her home.

He had always been her hero. Even when she couldn't understand him, had believed he'd never really loved her and had married her because he lusted after her, she'd never been able to topple him off the pedestal she'd created for him in her mind. Which was strange, considering everything.

Her throat tightened. There were things that had to be said. Now, in this softer, more receptive mood, surely he would listen?

He released his hold on her slowly, as if reassuring himself that she wouldn't fall in a wet and soggy heap, and bent to turn the bath taps on.

She reached out and touched his arm, and he straightened immediately at the slight contact, his breath bunching painfully in his lungs. Turning to her, his eyes narrowed with concern as he saw the glitter of unshed tears in her eyes.

'I'm sorry, Jake—'

'You're back now, no damage done,' he said quickly, his eyes sweeping her tense features. 'Don't waste your breath apologising.'

'I want to! Not just for taking off like that, but for everything else!' she cried, needing him to know how much she regretted what she'd done, needing him to understand why she'd done it. There had been too many thoughts left unspoken in the past, culminating in a total lack of communication. She should have tried harder to make him listen, make him understand. She could see that now.

'Shh.' He placed two fingers against her lips, silencing her, clamping his jaw tightly as he felt her mouth tremble beneath the gentle pressure, and stamping on the near-desperate urge to kiss her senseless as her lids fluttered closed, colour stealing into her flawless skin.

He couldn't listen to her raking over the past, hear her apologising for the act of adultery, promising it would never happen again. 'No post mortems,' he said thickly, taking his fingers from her mouth because touching her hadn't been one of his better ideas.

He tested the temperature of the water and turned off the taps. 'What you need is a warm bath and a hot drink.' He unbuttoned her soggy coat and removed it, his hands brisk, impersonal, his movements economical. Then he bent to tackle the laces of her walking shoes.

Looking down at his dark head, his wet hair plastered to his skull, Bella bit back a groan as the breath snagged in her lungs, making her heart race. Willing her fingers not to reach out and touch—not yet—she curved them sharply into her palms.

Maybe in a moment she could make her move…ask him to share the bath with her…? If the signs were right… If she had the courage…

Out of those three years of their marriage they'd spent a total of one hundred and thirty-one days together. She knew the tally exactly. She'd kept a record.

But she'd done her best, for the first couple of years at least, to make the most of their time together. And they'd shared a bath on many memorable occasions. Highly memorable occasions…

Her heart felt as if it were about to explode in her chest, her body too narrow to contain such tumultuous emotions. They'd been so good together—sexually at least—their need, their physical generosity, dovetailing perfectly, their passion carrying each other ever higher, reaching unbelievable realms of rapture.

Surely that spectacular closeness couldn't all be lost? There had to be something left they could build on. There had to be!

She stood like a rag doll as he undressed her. She could manage for herself perfectly well, but wasn't about to tell him so. Her damp sweater disposed of, he hooked impersonal fingers beneath the waistband of her leggings and dragged them down over her slender hips.

Bella shuddered as molten fire pooled deep down inside her. She wanted him so; her entire body was on fire for him, transformed into a silent, desperate cry of need, a plea for his lovemaking—a cry he surely must hear deep inside him, an inner cry of such longing she could almost hear it throbbing on the air.

His eyes slid over her body, lingering, dark colour slashing his hard, prominent cheekbones. And she knew, even before she heard the harsh rasp of his breath, that her body's silent cry of need had reached him, touched him....

Instinctively her hands went out, small palms sliding against the darkly stubbled, hewn contours of his face, long and elegant fingers resting on his temples, feeling the violence of the pulse there.

Jake moved sharply back, as if stung by a horde of angry hornets, his eyes bleak and mouth compressed as he delivered tersely, 'Shout if you need anything. I'll leave the door open.'

And he walked out on her, chilling indifference clearly stamped on the rigid lines of his broad back.

CHAPTER SIX

BACK in his room, Jake leaned against the closed door, teeth gritted, his head thrown back.

It had been a close call. Damn it, his body was still shaking. For several minutes his concern for her had been his salvation, helping him to strip her down as if he were a professional carer.

Only when she'd stood before him wearing nothing but those wicked wisps of lace that so lovingly cupped inviting, rosy-tipped breasts, and yet another scrap of lace-trimmed silk that covered...

He groaned, levering himself forward and shrugging out of his soaked jacket. He'd been doing fine until then. Just fine. But looking at her, remembering the passion and glory of their lovemaking, the meeting of their souls that had made them seem indivisible, had brought him to the point of reaching out for her, holding her, making her his again, and only his, for the rest of time.

But the smouldering, drowning invitation in her eyes when she'd slowly reached out and touched his face had brought him right back to his senses. Back with a hard, resounding crack.

Sex had been something she'd always been good at. Very good. As insatiable as he'd been himself where she was concerned.

So insatiable, indeed, she'd been hopping into bed

77

with that wife-stealing, wife-cheating bastard Maclaine whenever he'd been away. While he'd been working his guts out for them both, determined to secure their future, she'd been playing around with the man who'd been her lover all those years ago.

He'd keep that firmly to the forefront of his mind. It was a cast-iron, rock-solid defence against whatever acts of sorcery she dreamed up next!

It would be masochistic madness to weave the fabric of his life with hers again, naively hoping she would stay faithful. He couldn't take the heartbreak and disillusionment a second time around.

He'd been short on trust ever since his father—the man he'd loved, respected and, above all, trusted—had committed that ultimate betrayal, taking his own life and leaving his family to make what they could of the financial mess he'd left behind.

When Bella walked down the stairs, reluctantly dressed in flowing black silk trousers topped by a sleekly narrow white linen jacket worn over a black body, she was perfectly in control.

Watching as he'd walked out of that bathroom, she'd been devastated, hardly able to believe he'd been turning his back on the possibility of a mutual admission that they still cared for each other.

Because for a little while they'd been close, she knew they had, both physically and mentally. Closer than they'd been for a long time before their marriage had finally broken up. She'd felt it in her bones, felt the blossoming of hope in the quiet certainty of her heart.

The briefly wonderful hope had been cruelly shattered when he'd walked out of the door. He'd fought the growing closeness because he didn't want it. So be it. She could handle it, couldn't she? What was that old saying? You could take a horse to water but you couldn't make it drink...

Getting through to him when his mind was made up was impossible. She remembered now exactly when that fact of life had finally hit home...

Bella let herself into the Docklands apartment and thanked heaven for the central heating. The late-January evening was bitterly cold.

She removed her suit jacket and kicked off her shoes. And smiled. She'd been doing a lot of that just lately—smiling. Ever since Guy had made that proposition, given her existence a meaning that had been strangely absent during the two years and one month of her largely solitary marriage, she'd been feeling euphoric.

Dear, darling Guy!

They'd been heavily involved all day, and she felt pleasantly tired and thankful that she wasn't hungry because she had nothing in. Life had been too hectic since Guy had put forward his tempting offer to spare time for boring things like food shopping!

Deciding to listen to music, open a bottle of wine and come down from the high she now seemed permanently on, before getting an early night, she frowned as the phone in the living room shrilled out.

But it could be Guy. She lifted the receiver expectantly and Jake said, 'I'm at Heathrow. Can you fetch me, or shall I hire a car?'

He sounded desperately tired. 'I'm on my way,' she said quickly, her brows drawing together. He never flew in unexpectedly; he always let her know when he'd be home. She hoped there was nothing wrong.

'You work too hard,' she chided when she eventually drove them from the airport car park. He looked exhausted. 'Is there anything wrong?'

'Nothing that a few days of your home cooking and tender ministrations won't cure!' For a moment the teasing, sultry note was back in his voice, the slow smile he turned on her wiping the exhaustion from his face for a fleeting fraction of time.

Bella bit down on her lower lip, and concentrated fiercely on her driving. Now wasn't the right time to tell him she wouldn't be around. She could hardly let Guy down at this early stage of their renewed relationship.

Questions about his latest business trip elicited perfunctory answers, but the gist was that it had been highly satisfactory so she stopped asking and told herself he had obviously worked himself to a near standstill. She enquired instead, 'Are you hungry?'

'Ravenous.'

'Then we'll find a restaurant; I'm low on provisions. OK?'

'Fine. Somewhere low-key. Food, then bed. With you. Those are my priorities.'

Something in his voice told her that food came a very definite second on his list of two. Her whole body quivered. Their lovemaking was always spectacular, but his first night home after an absence that often stretched to weeks was sublime.

Without thinking—although later she was to wonder if it had been an unconscious wish to push the truth under his nose—she chose the small Italian restaurant in Canning Town where Guy had given her lunch and put his proposition to her. He often ate there, mostly in the evenings. His wife was again on a protracted visit to her parents, and as head of a thriving advertising agency he worked his socks off and couldn't face having to make himself a meal.

Not smart, the tiny restaurant was warm and friendly, the aroma of cooking appetising. They chose simply—pasta with spicy vegetables and a carafe of gutsy red wine.

Jake ate as if he were starving, as if he needed the wholesome, hot food, and the light was back in his eyes as he took her hand across the table and told her, 'I've missed you, Bel. Know something? You get more beautiful every time I see you. And know something else? I think I've made a decision—'

'Ah—the lovely Bella!' Whatever Jake had been about to tell her was cut short by the theatrical emergence of the proprietor from the kitchen. Carlo, Guy had introduced him over lunch that day. He had shiny black hair and a very big smile, and a tea-towel tied around his ample waist, tucked into his trousers at the back.

'You come again! My good friend Guy brings often new customers—people who want no frills, just good Italian food, home cooked. I tell him he has good taste—especially in his choice of so beautiful a companion!'

Bella felt something happen to her spine. Something like an army of ants scurrying up and down wearing needles of ice on their feet! Big on friendliness Carlo might be, but he was lamentably short on tact. He was seemingly oblivious to the black hostility in Jake's eyes as he beamingly asked, 'Is everything OK? *Dolce*, maybe?'

'Nothing.' Jake's reply was terse, his eyes hard as when they were alone again, he turned them on Bella's suddenly white face, raking them over her features as if he was trying to read what was going on in her mind. 'You come here often? You and Maclaine?'

'No, of course not.' The Italian had made it sound that way, but she'd only been here that one time. She twisted her napkin in her fingers. She was going to have to tell him now, and he wouldn't be pleased! In the past, whenever she'd mentioned Guy's name, Jake had changed the subject. He must have guessed, or heard, something about their former relationship. He was very possessive. 'I had lunch here with him. Once.'

It was then, precisely then, that he withdrew from her—quite possibly from their marriage. It was the beginning of the end, although she didn't know that then. She saw suspicion in his eyes, and did her best to counter it.

'I need to do something with my life, Jake. Can't you see that? Guy's offered me work; I've taken it.'

'Is that what you call it?'

Was he referring to her former modelling career? She knew he'd been happy when she'd given it up. As he'd said at the time, only half-jokingly, she suspected, he didn't like every Tom, Dick and Harry lusting after his much photographed wife.

Or did he mean something much darker?

'Jake, listen—' Her voice shook with the intensity of her need to make him hear her out, understand. 'This job, it's—'

'Leave it.' He was slapping banknotes down to cover the bill. 'If you want to work, go ahead. I wouldn't dream of asking you not to. If being my wife isn't "doing something with your life" then who am I to argue?'

He sounded indifferent.

He slept in the spare room that night, exhaustion his thin excuse. And over the following months he spent even more time away, and, when home with her, carefully avoided any mention of her job. And she, in turn, closed in on herself. Lack of communication became almost an art form...

Now the aroma of fresh coffee teased her nostrils as she walked through the kitchen. She ignored it, just as she made herself ignore the weakening effects of the past traumatic hours.

She'd used every last bit of her former expertise when she'd made herself up to match the clothes Evie's skulduggery had forced her to wear, carefully hiding her pallor and the lines of strain around her eyes. She needed confidence, control; she couldn't emerge from this nightmare with her self-respect intact without both held firmly in her hands.

She could hear him moving around in the living room. She took a deep breath, forced a serene expression and walked through.

Her eyes immediately went to him, lingering, drinking him in, as if her brain had no say in the matter. Changed into loose black denims topped by a rib-hugging black cashmere sweater, he should have looked menacing, intimidating. But he didn't. He looked heart-twistingly sexy.

She only had to look at him to experience the scorching, ravaging flames of desire, feel them wreaking their fiery onslaught through every tingling cell in her body. She dragged in a shuddery breath and prayed her inner turmoil didn't show.

He returned her riveted gaze with a slow, brooding appraisal, black eyes indolently skimming every line of her tautly held body as if he were stripping away the unlikely, elegant garments to the warm, suddenly trembling flesh beneath. And the air in the cosy little room became wildly over-heated, sizzling with churning sexual awareness.

Until he spoke, his cool, sardonic tone cutting through the atmosphere, one dark brow lifting upwards. 'I see you brought your designer labels along. Perfect choice for a winter break in the wilds of Wales.'

His sarcasm chilled her. 'Evie made a furtive last-minute substitution.' He wouldn't believe her. He wouldn't believe her if she said roses had thorns. And the twist of his long mouth told her she was correct in that assumption.

'You're slipping, Bella.' Glittering black eyes taunted her cruelly. 'You used to be such a good liar. Through three years of marriage you had me believing you were a faithful wife.'

Now, surely, was the time to put that right, to tell him that the fault was his, that she would never have left him if he had given her what she most needed, to explain exactly what that was.

'We need to discuss this,' she told him, her black-lashed, water-clear eyes huge with entreaty.

But he shook his head, frowning sharply. 'There's nothing to discuss—except how we're going to get through the next few days. It is Christmas, remember?'

He bent to tend the fledgling fire, and Bella swallowed the lump in her throat. Nothing to discuss. Their past, present and future relationship was too unimportant to waste breath on.

And of course she knew it was Christmas; she didn't need reminding.

It had become such a very special time of year for her, more than ordinarily so. Their whirlwind romance, followed by a Christmas Eve wedding. The first few days of their rapturous honeymoon spent in a quiet, rambling sixteenth-century inn tucked away in the Cotswolds. All the festive trimmings—roaring log fires, red-berried holly, even a light flurry of snow. Carol-singers, young voices crystal-clear in the frosty air, sparkly days and long nights filled with love and laughter. And talking.

Oh, how she'd talked, spilling out hopes she had never shared with anyone before. Hopes that had never been fulfilled.

'Yes, I remember,' she answered him, her voice flat. Over the past year anguish had been a constant companion. She'd thought she had learned to live with it, learned to cope. Clearly, she hadn't. 'I'll go and pour us some of that coffee.'

It was suddenly an effort to speak. The pain of disappointment hit her. She had so hoped, expected— yes, actually and foolishly expected…

'I'll do it. Stay here, get warm.' He was out of the room before she could argue. Not that she had the energy to argue about anything.

Slowly she moved to the fire and held her hands out to the warmth of the flames.

Reaction to this morning's hare-brained escapade was setting in. That was why she had been air-headed enough to imagine, for one single moment, that somehow they could work things out, that he did still care for her a little.

She didn't realise she'd been swaying on her feet until Jake thrust the tray he'd carried through down on a side table, put long-fingered hands on her shoulders and pressured her down onto the fireside chair.

Not that he needed to exert much pressure. Her legs felt as if they were made of water. He reached for the tray and placed it on her knees.

'Eat. Drink. I don't want you collapsing on me. I've no way of summoning medical aid, don't forget.'

Barely focusing, her eyes registered a china beaker of steaming coffee and a plate of lavishly buttered hot toast. His cool command made sense. Always the practical one, always able to find reasons why he couldn't give her what she craved.

She drank the coffee and forced down some of the toast, and managed a dull little, 'Thank you. I needed that.'

Jake removed the tray and said tersely, 'Too right, you did. You've actually got some colour back in your face that hasn't come out of a pot.'

Her cheeks, smooth as a rose petal, had a touch of pink beneath the translucent surface, and her lips had lost that worrying bluish tinge—formerly apparent in the whiteness around the coral lipstick she had so carefully painted on. He took up an unknowingly dominant stance in front of the hearth, breathed deeply and tried to make himself relax.

They were stuck out here, and there was no way he was going to spend Christmas in an ill-tempered, explosive atmosphere.

'I've a suggestion to make.' A stab of something fierce and hot knifed through him as her eyes winged up and locked with his. She had piled the silky mass of her black hair elegantly on the top of her head. The purity of the line from the crown of her head to the angle of her jaw, to the slender length of her neck, was sheer poetry. It made him ache.

He clenched his hands in the pockets of his jeans. And tried again. 'I suggest we try to make the best of the situation.' Suddenly it was vitally important to him that she agree to a truce. He cleared his throat and continued with a careful lack of inflection. 'We're stuck here. Whether we like it or not. In my opinion, it wouldn't make a whole heap of sense to spend Christmas glowering at each other from opposite ends of the room.'

The clear luminosity of her eyes cut to his soul. She looked as though she was hanging on every word, like a child who was waiting to hear the details of a long-awaited treat. Despite the veneer of elegant sophistication those expressive eyes made her look so trusting, so innocent.

Yet she was light years away from innocence, he reminded himself with a brutality he suddenly felt was very necessary.

'So why don't we forget the past for a couple of days, call a truce and behave like rational adults?'

He knew he'd sounded harsher than he'd meant to, and instantly regretted it as he watched her head droop, those eyes not intent on him now, but on the long-fingered hands that lay clasped in her lap.

He held his breath, expecting the retaliation of total non-compliance or, at best, the silent withdrawal that had tainted the last year of their marriage. Though he, too, had been guilty in that respect, he recognised now.

'Sounds like sense to me, too.' Bella did her best to sound like the rational adult he'd suggested she try to be. The spiky lump in her throat was her own fault. Stupid of her to have thought, at first, that he was trying to tell her that they should use this time to try to resurrect their marriage, work on their shattered relationship, talk things out.

But his harshly impatient suggestion that they forget the past, just for a day or so, had knocked that fantasy on the head.

He wanted to forget that they'd ever meant anything to each other. She had no option but to play it his way, and she knew that if she were to survive the next few days without making a shameful fool of herself she would have to convince her stupid heart that their separation was the first step in rectifying a bad mistake. Perhaps even steel herself to mention divorce.

She got to her feet, and challenged him. 'I won't glower, if you won't. And, to make it easier, shall we dress the tree? There's one in the kitchen, in case you hadn't noticed.'

'I could hardly have failed, since I almost poked my eye out on the darned thing a couple of times.'

She hadn't left out a single thing when she'd made her minute arrangements for the 'surprise' reunion! Jake stamped on the thought. No past, no recriminations, simply a polite coexistence—on the surface, anyway. He was working on it. He had to. It had been his idea, hadn't it? He'd do anything to make the next few days as amicable as they could be. Polite formality was definitely the only safe atmosphere to aim for.

He would do anything to avoid any attempts on her part to affect a reconciliation. That had to be why she'd set this up. And she had enough witchery at her command to make him follow his heart, ignore the sullied past and resume their marriage.

He would fight to the last breath to avoid putting himself through that kind of hell again.

'I'll carry it through; you decide where you think it would look best.'

In the end they both agreed the tree would look perfect in the alcove at the side of the inglenook.

'Out of the way of any flying sparks,' Jake approved. 'Shall you hang the bits and bobs, or shall I?'

'Why don't we do it together?' Immediately the question was out she regretted it. It sounded pushy. Togetherness was something that had been missing from their relationship for a long time now. No chance of finding it again either. He didn't want to find it so they wouldn't. What Jake wanted, Jake got.

'One of us has to fix lunch,' he told her, smoothly glossing over her mistake. 'Breakfast, for me, was a non-event, and yours—two bites of toast just now— doesn't count. I'll forage in the kitchen while you deck the tree.'

It wasn't cowardice, he told himself grimly as he jerked the fridge door open and glared at the brimming contents. He needed to keep things cool, polite—if only superficially. It was the only way he could get through this without his emotions ending up in chaos.

He pulled a slab of cold roasted beef from the well-stocked shelves and began to slice at it for sandwiches. He had nothing to fear, he reminded himself. Not a damn thing. He had the protection of her past infidelities, hadn't he? Not to mention the reinforcement of her latest devious behaviour—the setting up of this farce.

Jake eyed the mound of meat he'd hacked with grim hostility. The slices were distinctly uneven, ragged, as if someone had set about the cold roast with an axe. And he wondered why he had to keep reminding himself of the reasons for keeping her at arm's length.

After what she'd done to him, to their marriage, he would have thought his heart would have grown a protective shell a mile thick, the reasons for keeping her at a firm distance permanently engraved on his brain.

He shouldn't have to work on it.

It shouldn't have to be so hard!

If he allowed her back into his life he would deserve all he got. Heartbreak. Forever wondering if she was sneaking off to be with Maclaine whenever his back was turned. He couldn't face the pain of that again.

CHAPTER SEVEN

AT FIRST Bella had been all fumbling thumbs and deep and nervy embarrassment at having left herself wide open to that rebuff. Play the game—for a game it surely was—as if they were mere acquaintances, politely resigned to spending time together; that was the way Jake wanted it. So that was the way he'd get it, she'd told herself firmly. She would demonstrate that she could play the game as well as he. Better, even!

But soon the glittering festive baubles had entranced her: gold, silver and scarlet, glimmering and twinkling amongst the dark evergreen branches, swags of shiny red beads roping in and out of the pine-fragrant foliage. It all made her forget, for a few precious minutes, the hurting hatefulness of her situation.

She was standing back, her head tipped to one side, wondering if the effect she'd achieved looked as good as she thought it did, when Jake walked back in from the kitchen, carrying a loaded tray.

'How does it look? OK?' She didn't turn after that initial over-the-shoulder glance. Still caught up in almost child-like excitement, she took Jake's long moment of intense silence for consideration of her artistic efforts. The result had to be a bit odd or he wouldn't be taking so long to offer an opinion. 'Did I put too much on? Is it over the top? I've never dressed a tree before.'

Jake put the tray down on the table, his mouth curving cynically. For a few moments back there she'd had him entranced. Standing there, a great and glittering gold star clutched in her hands, her lovely face radiating pleasure, there'd been no sign of the sleek 'top model' sophistication he'd always associated with Bella. The breathy, whispery excitement in her voice had almost fooled him, too.

He clattered plates. 'Never dressed a tree? Pull the other one! Then come and eat.'

So she wasn't even to be allowed the fleeting distraction of doing something pleasurable for the very first time. And why did he have to believe that every time she opened her mouth a lie came out?

She swung round on her heels. It was time he got a few things straight. She didn't lie, for one.

Tossing the glittery star on the tabletop, she told him levelly, 'It happens to be the truth. If you can't believe it, then that's your tough luck. Not mine.'

Still unloading the tray, he gave her a penetrating look. Maybe he was taking distrust too far. Distrust had been stamped on his soul when his father had taken his life. Of his parents, his father had been his rock, a larger than life figure he had respected as well as loved. The loss of financial security and the huge debts his father had left behind had been as nothing compared with that final betrayal.

To begin with, he'd believed he had learned to trust again with Bella. But infidelity made a mockery of marriage vows, turned them into lies. Infidelity was a sure-fire way of killing trust.

He pulled out a chair for her and took one for himself on the opposite side of the table. 'So tell me about it. Didn't your parents let you help dress the tree when you were a kid?'

She took her chair, shrugged very slightly. 'It's not important.'

'Probably not.' He pushed a plate of sandwiches towards her. 'But it would help pass the time. And, now I come to think of it, you've told me very little about your past.'

Pass the time. It stretched endlessly before her, arid, awkward and painful. She blinked rapidly. She would not cry. She took a sandwich of doorstep proportions, refused the soggy-looking salad garnish he'd prepared.

'I thought, for the purposes of Christmas peace and goodwill, we had to ignore the past.' She threw his cool stricture back in his face. The little rebellion helped to smother the feeling of hurt. She calmly eyed the thing on her plate and wondered if she could open her mouth wide enough to take a bite.

'The distant past doesn't count.' He found himself approving this new spark of defiance. And, watching her, he had to fight to stop himself from grinning like a clown. If he'd been asked to describe the marital meals she'd used to go to such endearingly endless trouble to prepare for him, he would have said elegant. And beautiful to look at. Ten out of ten for presentation, and two out of ten for hunger-quelling content.

Right now she was having difficulty hiding her dismay. He hadn't gone out of his way to produce such massive, untidy offerings. He couldn't have been concentrating on what he was doing.

'OK.' She capitulated, and reached for a knife to cut the sandwich into smaller, more manageable pieces. 'I suppose it wouldn't help the festive spirit much if we both sat here in gloomy silence. I'll go along with you, and try to avoid contentious subjects. But I warn you, I'm not going to pussy-foot around, double-checking everything before it trips off my tongue, like a reformed trollop at a vicar's tea party.'

He did grin then, but hid it behind the rim of his wineglass. An excellent vintage claret, he'd noted back in the kitchen, twisting the corkscrew with cynical ferocity. She'd spared no expense to get the party moving, to find the right mood!

He caught the thought, examined it. Was he being unfair? Was she in some kind of trouble? Had she engineered this time together because she needed his help? It was something to think about. Maybe if she relaxed enough she would tell him the truth.

'So?' he prompted gently, watching her long, narrow hands as she cut into the thick, crusty bread and the filling of hacked meat. He wondered why she didn't push it fastidiously aside and float out to prepare a medallion of tenderloin on a bed of unidentifiable leaves. She was obviously trying hard to please.

'So Dad thought Christmas was a waste of money, right? But Mum always did her best to make sure Evie and I had a package to open on Christmas morning.

Granted, money was in short supply—but he didn't even make an effort, and wouldn't let us try, either.'

She chewed reflectively on a piece of her sandwich; the meat was wonderfully tender, spiced up with just the right amount of mustard. His sandwiches were no way as inedible as they looked.

'I like to think he wasn't a Scrooge by nature, but acted like one because it upset him to think he couldn't give his family everything they wanted.'

She looked so earnest, Jake thought, watching her closely. Somehow he couldn't bring himself to say what was on his mind—that any father who didn't make the effort to find some way of making Christmas special for his kids didn't deserve to have any. Let her keep her manufactured delusions if they helped her.

'Dad was mostly out of work, and we were always on the move,' she was telling him, long fingers idly stroking the stem of her wineglass now. 'He always thought the grass would be greener in the next county or town. It never was, though. Things just seemed to go from bad to worse. Smaller flats in seedier areas. And moving meant Mum had to keep finding new jobs to make ends meet. Sometimes she couldn't. Things got really tough then.'

Her mother had never complained. Bella wondered if she'd inherited those doormat genes, making her willing to let Jake call all the shots during the time they'd lived together.

Unconsciously she shook her head. Now wasn't the time to delve into cause and effect.

Jake said, his voice surprisingly gentle, 'I remember you telling me your parents were separated, and your mother settled in New Zealand with her widowed sister.'

'Yes, but Mum going out to live with Auntie May came much later. She wouldn't have dreamed of leaving us until Evie and I were both on our feet. But Dad walked out on the lot of us when I was fourteen. We stayed put, then, and for a couple of years the three of us had our first settled home. A two-bedroom flat above a greengrocer's in a backstreet in Newcastle. Downmarket, but home.'

She was twisting the glass now. Jake expected the contents to spill out at any moment. There was a lot of tension there, waiting to be released.

'It must have been about that time I knew what I wanted out of life.'

She wasn't looking at him; her expression told him she was in another world. But at least she was trying to share it with him. Funny how they'd never really talked, either of them, never delved deeply enough to find out what made each other tick.

Too busy making love, discovering each other physically to begin with. And then, after the initial honeymoon stage, he'd been too busy. Full-stop.

Not sure that he should want to, but feeling driven to know, Jake asked, 'And what was that?'

Christmas every day of the year? Everything her deprived childhood had seemingly put out of reach? Designer clothes, jewels, fast cars and slow, sybaritic holidays in far-flung places?

Heaven knew, she'd earned enough in her own right to indulge every whim, and the Docklands home he'd provided on their marriage had been glamorous enough to negate the memories of any number of back-street flats.

Yet it hadn't been enough. His love hadn't been enough. Being his wife, in spite of all the financial advantages—like not having to work for her extremely comfortable living—had become a bore. So much so that she had sought forbidden excitement with her former lover.

Bella, glancing across at him between dark and tangled lashes, saw the ferocity darkening his face and made up her mind. Conscious, suddenly, that she was in danger of snapping the stem of her glass, she made herself loosen up, unknotting her fingers and lifting the brimming glass to her mouth.

They'd agreed not to raise any contentious spectres from the past—but it might dent his huge ego, and certainly wouldn't hurt him, to know that one of the things she had most wanted—not the most important, but important nevertheless—was something else he'd resolutely refused to give her. She had nothing to lose because she'd already lost everything that mattered to her.

'I did tell you once, but I guess you didn't listen. You never listened to what I said if it wasn't what you wanted to hear. Eventually I stopped saying anything important.' She looked him straight in the eye and knew a moment's vindication when she watched his dark brows pull down as her shot hit home.

She gave a small shrug, slender shoulders lifting elegantly beneath the beautifully styled white jacket.

'I wanted a proper home and a loving family to share it with,' she said with a touch of cool defiance.

She looked at her empty glass with a glimmer of surprise and put it down. Swallowing wine as if it were water wouldn't help. She sat rigidly upright in her chair, her hands knotted in her lap, and added, 'Nothing grand, just a homey place with a garden, and fields and woods around for the children to play in.' And a husband who was home, sharing the ups and downs of family life, the two of them growing closer as the years went by, not further and further apart until they were like strangers.

She frowned unconsciously, and tacked on tartly, 'No grimy backstreets, litter and graffiti everywhere—some place where it was safe to walk, with fresh air to breathe. A modest enough dream, but one I valued.'

She'd said enough. Perhaps too much. The silence from him was like a shock. But, oddly, she felt unburdened, lighter. She wasn't so self-centred that his refusal to even think about the occasional suggestions she'd made regarding a future move out of the City would have made her decide their marriage wasn't worth keeping.

But she wouldn't think about that; she couldn't afford to. Dwelling on what had gone so badly wrong wouldn't help her to get through the next few days, or keep up the pretence that they were mere acquaintances.

She swept to her feet and began to gather the lunch things together, and told him politely, very politely, 'I'll clear away. Would you mind fixing the star to the top of the tree? I couldn't reach.'

With the kitchen door closed firmly behind her, Bella released a long, shuddery sigh. She wanted to kill Evie for putting her in this situation! Kitty, too, for her part in it! The only thing that gave her any consolation whatsoever was knowing that this place, fully and lavishly provisioned, would have cost them at least an arm and a couple of legs apiece!

Their intentions had been good, though; she had to give them that. But they were living in cloud-cuckoo-land if they thought that this enforced and probably prolonged contact would have the desired results.

Jake didn't even like her any more. He didn't trust her. He would sooner handcuff himself to a baboon for the rest of his life than take her back!

Tears rushed to her eyes. She blinked them away and sniffed ferociously, took the tray to the sink and did the dishes, then collected the clothes they'd worn earlier in the blizzard and pushed them into the washer-drier. Anything to keep busy, keep out of the way of the man she had loved and lost.

From behind the closed door Jake could hear the clink of china. At odds with his chaotic emotions, Bella was prosaically washing the dishes. The sheer unexpectedness of what she'd said had robbed him of speech.

Of course he'd listened when she'd dreamily told him of what she envisaged for their future. Late-night lover-talk, he'd thought it, with her hair splayed against the pillows like a black silk shawl.

He could remember it now, too vividly for comfort—cocooned together in the secret love-cave of the four-poster bed in that quaint old Cotswolds inn where they'd spent the first Christmas of their honeymoon. Her eyes dreamy, romantic, her voice soft and sweet with talk of country cottages, roses round the door, children—their children—fantasy children she'd created for him.

His fingers stroking her hair, her face, the trembling starting up inside him again, his hand sliding down to the sensual swell of her breasts, his mouth covering hers, silencing her. His love for her, his need to drown himself yet again in the perfection of her overwhelming him...

The groan that was torn from him was driven. Oh, God, if only he could wipe his mind clean of all memories! He gritted his teeth, making himself backtrack to what she had actually said, recalling the defiance, the tension in the way she'd said it.

True, in the first couple of years of their marriage she had sometimes mentioned the possibility of moving to the country and starting a family. But she hadn't made a song and dance about it, and had quietly accepted it when he had decided they should stay where they were.

He'd assumed she meant some place tamed and tidy, chocolate-box rural. And he'd had damn good reasons for not wanting to alter his *modus operandi* at that time. He'd explained that a move, putting down roots and starting a family, was out of the question. For the time being anyway. He hadn't known how much—and why—she'd wanted what she called a proper home.

Why hadn't she told him? In view of her deprived childhood—and that was something else she hadn't told him about—he would have understood. And, understanding, he would have set about doing something about it.

He had loved her more than life, and would have done anything to make her happy.

Were there other things he didn't know about her? Things she'd kept back, kept hidden? His jaw tightened. Damn it, he'd been her husband; he'd had a right to know!

And yet he hadn't made his motives clear, had he? At least, not the underlying motives. The sudden thought washed his mind with icy clarity. Had he been too arrogant, too driven by his own needs, too intent on doing things his way to share the essence of himself with her?

He didn't feel comfortable with himself about that. His face darkened, tightened, and self-disgust turned into a hard, sharp lump inside him. He had watched her become more withdrawn, more closed in on herself, and had done nothing about it, preferring to assume that it was nothing important. After all, so he had told himself, he'd given her every material advantage any woman could possibly want, and their lovemaking had still been as explosively rapturous as ever.

But that hadn't been enough. She'd been seeing Maclaine when he was away and had agreed to work with him again. She had been sleeping with him again. All the signs had pointed to it.

He could hear her moving about in the next room. He'd go in there and fetch her. Tell her he'd been wrong about forgetting the past while they were trapped here together. It wouldn't let itself be forgotten!

So they'd talk, go into this thing, thrash it all out until there was nothing left to know. And maybe, along the way, he'd discover whether he'd been responsible for driving her back into Maclaine's arms.

He was on his way to do just that when he heard the sound of a tractor. He turned quickly on the balls of his feet and strode to the window.

The machine had already crested the brow of the hill, the snow-plough attachment steadily but surely clearing the track towards the cottage.

This was his way out. Out of here, back to civilisation, where he could arrange for transport out for Bella. And then he could get on with his life, let her get on with hers. They would go their separate ways again.

His way out. If he wanted to take it.

He grabbed his sheepskin from the hook on the back of the kitchen door and walked out into the cold winter afternoon.

CHAPTER EIGHT

BELLA remembered noticing storage heaters upstairs, and went up and switched them on. At least the bedrooms would be less arctic tonight.

Tonight. Her heart filled with a painful mixture of yearning and bleak despair. Another endless, restless night, knowing Jake was in the next room, a few yards away, yet so distant from her he might as well be on the far side of the moon.

There had been moments when she'd really thought he still cared, but that had been nothing more than self-delusion, wishful thinking. She put it down to his determination to get through the next few days with as little friction as possible. He wouldn't want a rerun of this morning's crazy escape attempt, or hysterics or sulks.

Steeling herself, she started down the stairs to join him again, deeply envying his ability to cut his losses, write the three years of their marriage off as an unfortunate mistake and get on with his life. She wished she cared so little about him that she could do the same.

Part of the way down she heard the laboured sound of a tractor. She froze, unable to believe it at first, then ran back up to the tiny window at the head of the staircase and peered out.

Jake, still shrugging into his coat, was pushing

through the snow towards the tractor. It had already cleared most of the track. Numb, clutching onto the window-sill, Bella watched as Jake reached the vehicle.

She could imagine the conversation going on between him and the driver. He would be asking for a lift out of here, explaining that his car wasn't functioning. And as Jake reached into an inside pocket she turned away, trudging down the stairs on leaden legs.

They'd be out of here before nightfall—or he would, at least. Jake would fix that. He always managed to get his own way.

She wanted to put back her head and howl, and the urge to weep her heart out was almost irresistible. But she wouldn't do either of those things. She wouldn't let herself be such a fool.

'The cavalry's arrived!' Five minutes later he walked back in, bringing a wave of crisp frosty air with him.

That was why she was shivering all over, Bella decided, and forced herself to sound interested. 'So I saw. We can't be as isolated as we thought we were.'

The snow plough was back in operation again. The noise was growing louder as the driver approached the cottage.

'How on earth did he know we were snowed-up here?' She felt too dead inside to really care, but it was something to say, a way of masking her foolish inner dread at the coming parting.

But perhaps the ending of their enforced stay was a blessing, she decided dully, doing her best to convince herself. Being with him only brought back all the pain of wanting him, the mental and physical agony of knowing he could hardly bear to be anywhere around her.

The only real question was, would Jake go back in the cab with the driver alone, or would he take her with him? He was looking mightily pleased with himself, and was making no effort to remove his coat.

Which meant he was intending to leave any time now. She thought about the clothes still in the drier, the packing she'd have to do, the brightly burning fire which would have to burn down to ashes before it was safe to be left, and knew Jake wouldn't hang around until everything was sorted. Neither, in all probability, would the tractor driver.

Jake was going to leave her behind, and was looking insultingly happy about it. Grinning!

'The owners of the cottage got in touch with him. He farms in the locality and the council uses him to clear some of the lanes. They—the owners—didn't want their holiday tenants to feel snowed in and abandoned.'

She watched him walk to the fire, hold his hands to the flames. Even though his back was firmly turned to her she knew he was still looking pleased with himself. He couldn't wait to wash his hands of her!

As the tractor reached the cottage, did an ungainly three-point turn then stopped, Jake swung round and walked to the door, obviously leaving without even saying goodbye, and Bella said rawly, 'I take it you're going back with the driver. Would you ask him to wait while I get ready to leave, too?'

She simply couldn't bear the thought of being here

alone, with these new and hurtful memories to add to all the rest. It was too much heavy baggage to have to carry through the long, lonely years that stretched ahead.

Jake turned, scanning her features with narrowed eyes. If the arrival of the snow plough had surprised him, it had obviously shocked her. Ruined all her carefully laid plans. He could read the dredging disappointment in her beautiful eyes.

Well, he was going to let her get her own way. He hadn't known why he'd done it, not at first. But now he did. They were going to talk the whole thing through, and for that they needed time and space.

He needed to learn her secrets—if she had any more to divulge—discover exactly how and why their marriage had failed.

Because then, and only then, would he be able to put it all behind him and attain the freedom he needed to get on with the rest of his life, unfettered by memories and regrets.

Knowing that the prospect of freedom from the spell she'd cast on him the very first time he'd seen her had to be responsible for his present adrenalin-high, he made no attempt to keep the underlying hint of laughter from his voice as he told her, 'We're not going anywhere for a couple of days. Put the kettle on; we have a guest.'

The driver of the tractor was a wiry little man, swamped by a thick waxed jacket and a big red knitted hat. His name was Evan Evans, and he insisted on removing his boots.

His knitted socks were red, too, Bella noted, hurrying to make the hot drink Jake had offered, her heart winging with a great surge of happiness she desperately tried to suppress.

Jake could have left; there'd been nothing to stop him. Except the desire to stay?

But she mustn't think like a naive teenager, she chided herself as she moved round the kitchen, the murmur of masculine voices coming from the other room a backdrop to her thoughts.

He had no desire to be with her—hadn't he made that crystal-clear? For the past twelve months their marriage hadn't been either one thing or another. He probably wanted to get everything sorted out, discuss divorce, tidy everything up.

The cold almost certainty of that left her feeling physically and mentally drained. Yet hope lingered, a feeble but stubbornly burning flame at the back of her mind. She didn't want hope, not when it would surely turn out to be false.

Telling herself to keep her chaotic emotions in check, she made hot chocolate for the men and found a tin of biscuits. She opened it and put it beside the mugs on the kitchen table, then called them through.

'There's lovely, isn't it?' Evan picked up his mug and cradled it in mittened hands. 'Just what I needed.' He refused to sit, blowing on his drink to cool it, and Bella handed Jake his mug, careful not to look at his face. He might see those futile hopes warring with the bleak certainties in her eyes.

'So I'll phone the recovery service and give them your details, and ask them to bring the part out on Boxing Day. Is it set on spending Christmas you are?

Snow or no snow?' Evan finished his drink. 'It's a tidy enough place.' He glanced around him, his eyes twinkling with open appreciation as they rested on Bella. 'Don't blame you, mind. Do the same in your shoes! Though who'd go vandalising your car is beyond me.'

He scratched the side of his head and the knitted cap rose higher, looking, Bella decided half-hysterically, like a melting church steeple.

'Don't worry about it,' Jake said smoothly. 'We're very grateful for your help.'

Bella tried to analyse his tone. Satisfaction, or amusement? She couldn't decide which. And Evan was getting ready to leave.

'Missus'll be wondering where I've got to. We've got all the family back with us for Christmas, as usual. Five grandchildren in all. Little imps! Mind you—' bright brown eyes twinkled beneath the scarlet of the rearing hat '—Christmas wouldn't be the same without their racket, would it? *And*—' he stressed the word heavily, smiling broadly '—I'm doing Santa duty again. Each year I tell myself it's the last time I'm dressing up in all that stuff. Seems I never learn!'

Bella watched him go, accompanied by Jake, to find his boots, and envied him. She closed her eyes and desperately envied all the families happily getting ready to celebrate this special season. And when Jake joined her there were tears in her eyes.

'Why didn't you go with him?' she demanded thickly. Attack was the best form of defence—defence against the reckless need to hurl herself into his arms and beg him to fall in love with her again, to want her with the almost obsessive need that had driven them both ever since the very first time they'd met.

To beg him to take the hurt away.

'Because I've finally reached the conclusion that we need to talk. We've spent a whole year avoiding each other and it doesn't make any kind of sense. We've got to find a way to put the past behind us. We both need to be free to get on with our lives.'

'Yes, I see.' She turned away, trying to conceal the hurt. She'd guessed his motives for staying on here, but that didn't make it any easier to bear. He was going to suggest divorce.

'But not right now. There's plenty of time. A couple of days,' he said, his voice softening. There were tough questions to be asked, tough decisions to be made. It wouldn't be easy on either of them. And right now she looked so vulnerable, almost utterly defeated, and that wasn't like the Bella he knew.

The range and depth of the sweeping wave of compassion he felt for her came as a shock. For a moment it took his breath away.

Suddenly restless he suggested, 'So why don't we try to relax, get a breath of air before it gets dark?' He watched the graceful tilt of her head as she turned huge, questioning eyes to him. 'I don't mean a repeat of this morning's marathon!' he assured her, reliving the long minutes of frantic concern when he'd been afraid he'd never find her, wondering what that reckless journey of hers out into the blizzard had been meant to prove.

He pushed a log further onto the glowing embers with a booted foot, needing action of some kind, no matter how small, and then added more harshly than he'd intended, 'It was a suggestion, that's all. You don't have to come. But I need air.'

'I'll be two minutes.' Relief washed through her, washed away the tension, making her body feel light as air as she went to the kitchen. The terrible conversation that would lead to the legal ending of their marriage was to be postponed. Maybe, later, she'd find the strength from somewhere to handle it with dignity.

She fished the clothes from the drier and sped up the stairs, casting aside all that out-of-place elegance. She dressed hurriedly in the leggings and sweater, clean and still warm from the dryer, and pulled his bulky Aran jumper on over the top because her own coat was still damp.

Her hair had come adrift. She gave it an impatient look in the mirror, and sped out of the room and down the stairs. She didn't have time to fiddle.

'Just ten minutes. Right?' Jake asked as she joined him.

'Right.' The smile she gave him was unpremeditated. But the look of approval in his eyes as he swept them over her altered, casual appearance had warmed away all her cool defences.

And his suggestion had been a good one. The air was stingingly cold, but it made her feel suddenly alive. Vitally, joyously alive—something she hadn't experienced since they'd separated. The misty orange sun was low in the washed-out blue of the sky, casting long, dark shadows on the glittering snow.

Bella quickened her pace, revelling in the way her

blood seemed to positively bounce through her veins, until Jake gently hauled her back, the strength of his hand tight and protective on her arm.

'Hey! Cool it. The track's slippery as hell now. A broken leg we can do without!'

Eyes wary, her heart beating skittishly, she fell in step beside him, expecting him to release her arm as soon as he'd successfully reined her in. He didn't. He held her more tightly, gathering her towards him, tucking her closely to the side of his body.

Every nerve-end stood to attention, and her stomach lurched. Didn't he know what his touch did to her? Had he forgotten that she only had to be near him to go up in flames? Were his memories of all they had been to each other so easily, so callously erased?

Her eyes fixed on the now-glassy surface of the compacted snow on the track ahead, she battled to find something to say, something to defuse the sharply coiling sexual tension that seemed to be eating her alive.

She came up with, 'So you didn't tell Mr Evans who had vandalised your car.' Her voice was shaky. She tried to turn the wobble into a laugh. 'The poor guy will spend months wondering if he's going to wake up in the morning and find no wheels on his tractor. He'll be looking at perfectly innocent local lads—wondering which of them has developed the urge to sneak around putting other people's vehicles out of commission!'

Jake stopped, his black eyes glittering down at her. 'What would you have had me say?' he wanted to know. 'That my wife arranged a little sabotage?' He turned back towards the cottage, his grip on her arm tightening cruelly.

Bella dug her heels into the compacted snow, dragged her arm from his grasp and flung at him, 'I had nothing to do with it—nothing!' Her eyes narrowed, anger whipping colour into her cheeks, she planted her hands on her hips and shouted, 'I don't know which makes me madder—what Evie did or you refusing to believe she did it!'

Jake quirked an eyebrow and had difficulty keeping his mouth straight. She looked incredibly fragile, and endearingly feisty. A kitten spitting tacks at a tiger! And he knew that nothing, short of kissing her until she was breathless, would stop the tirade.

Something deep inside him shuddered. Kissing her would be a bad mistake, the worst he could make.

'If she was here right now I'd throttle her!' Her mouth compressed against her teeth as she spat out tightly, 'What gives her the right to interfere? She's done it before, in a big way. It turned out OK that time—but this time it's an unmitigated disaster!'

She pushed the hair out of her eyes with an angry swipe. 'I'm going in. I'm cold! And I'm sick of the company I'm being forced to keep!'

She stamped along the track. She wasn't cold, she was burning with rage. At him. At Evie. At every mortal thing! And she was sick of him thinking she didn't know the meaning of truth!

She felt her feet go from under her at the very same time she heard Jake's warning shout, felt him reach out for her—but too late. She was floundering in the huge pile of snow shifted by the snow plough, all the breath knocked out of her lungs, with Jake's big body sprawled on top of her because he'd lost his footing trying to prevent her from falling.

He saw her eyes go wide, diamond lights glittering in those water-clear depths, and knew she hadn't hurt herself. There was nothing wrong with her except for a bad case of temper.

Her silky black hair was spread against the soft white snow, her kissable lips parted, her breasts straining against him as she tried to recapture her breath. Sudden desire for her—the desire that had never died no matter how hard he'd tried to kill it—hit him like a hammer-blow. Blood pounded through his veins, throbbing at his temples.

She was magic, and, as ever, he was under her spell. Whatever she was, whatever she had done, he wanted her, needed her...

Bella glared up at him, at his face just inches from hers. The utter humiliation of taking a header into the snow added to her rage. She wanted to tell him to let her up, get off her, but hadn't got her breath back. She did the only thing she could—grabbed a handful of snow and pushed it in his face.

Jake brushed the snow away with what to Bella seemed like contempt; the suddenly hard line of his mouth was a fearful thing.

He was fighting for control. Her puny attack invited retaliation—and he knew how to subdue her, what it would take. A long, slow mastery, first of her senses and then of her body—a slow and very deliberate and highly satisfactory easing of the tension, an assuaging of the long, aching emptiness that was hunger—taking her with him to where they could both find the sweet solace of physical release.

But that wasn't the way, he knew that, and as his mind won over his physical needs he pushed his hands beneath the bulk of the sweater she wore, his own sweater, and began to tickle her remorselessly. His strong features relaxed into a grin as the anger went out of her lovely face and she giggled and writhed and hiccuped beneath his relentless fingers.

'Right, madam!' He let his hands slide away, giving in at last to her squeals for mercy, pulling himself up onto his knees. 'Punishment over. Don't push snow in my face again or you'll know what to expect!' The impossibly inviting yet potentially damaging situation was defused, or so he thought.

Until her eyes met his. Sparkling with the laughter-tears that spangled and tangled her long dark lashes, they drew him closer, ever closer, inviting, promising... An irresistible promise fatally reinforced by the curved, parted lips...

Jake groaned silently, trying to force his body's response out of existence—the incredible hardening, tightening, the pooling of scalding heat in his loins, the thudding beat of his heart, the desperate need for her and only her.

If he took what was being offered he knew he would be doomed—binding himself to her again, with the knowledge of her previous unfaithfulness, the mental agony of wondering if she was sneaking off to be with Maclaine whenever his back was turned eating into him like acid.

The mental reminder of her lover got him to his feet. He brushed the powdery snow from his clothes, his eyes glinting narrowly as she made no move to get to her own feet. She simply held out her hands to him, her eyes still dancing with laughter. Or wicked, wilful, wanton promise?

He took her hands and hauled her unceremoniously out of the bank of snow, the familiar sensation as her slender fingers curled around his slamming into his body. To smother it he said, with what he hoped would come over as bland indifference, 'I never knew you were so ticklish. You live and learn.'

'Well, we never did play games, did we?' Still slightly breathless, her voice emerged huskily and she gave him an unknowingly provocative glance from beneath tangled lashes.

'As I recall, we did.' His face went hard. 'The games we played in bed were mind-blowing.' He turned from her, covering the last few yards to the cottage quickly.

Bella scurried after him. 'I didn't mean that!'

Why dredge up all that had been so wonderful, so right between them, and throw it in her face? To her intense aggravation she felt herself blushing as he turned those narrowed black eyes on her.

She looked so flustered, so innocent. With a harsh inner voice he reminded himself that she wasn't. 'No? You could have won an Olympic gold, the games you played. You must have had an excellent coach. Just Maclaine? Or were there others?'

For a moment his words didn't sink in. And when they did she didn't believe it—and then she did. Oh, she believed it, all right. He would hold her relationship with Guy against her for the rest of his life, not understanding it, twisting it, making it ugly and unrecognisable with his total lack of trust—the way he could think the very worst of her. No room for doubts, questions. No fair hearing. Simply a blind and devastatingly insulting acceptance of her non-existent infidelity!

She stared at him, her face drained of colour, her eyes wide and dark with pain. 'Guy has never been my lover.' Her eyes dropped from his, her soft mouth trembling. The purity of her profile tugged at his heart, making it ache. 'Though there seems little point in telling you. You won't believe me.'

Too right, he wouldn't.

Before he'd met her, her relationship with Maclaine had been common knowledge. The two of them—with the bastard's wife of the moment making an uneasy third—had been the subject of endless behind-the-hand gossip, according to Alex Griffith, the long-time friend who had persuaded him to go to that fateful party. He had no reason to doubt his friend's word. He would have had no reason whatsoever for inventing such a story.

Neither of them had ever discussed her long-running affair. She, naturally enough, had never brought the subject up, and he had done his best to forget it. She'd been his—his alone—and he hadn't been able to bear to think of her sharing such intimacies with another man. It had made him sick with jealousy. So he'd pushed it to the back of his mind, the present and the future all that mattered.

But the present and the future had been irreversibly soured when he'd walked in and found them in each others arms. Though the rot had set in long before that, when he'd discovered she'd been seeing the other man and had gone back to work for his agency.

He took his bunched hands from his pockets and pushed on the door, and she said, her voice shaky but challenging, 'There was only one man before you. And that was a short-lived disaster.'

He turned to look at her. It was a mistake. The huge eyes were pleading, begging for his trust, and she was trying to blink back tears, biting down on her lip to still the trembling. The desire to stop the trembling with his own mouth was strong enough to make him shake.

He pulled in a ragged breath, forcibly reminding himself of her acting abilities, of the manipulative, devious side of her nature which had hatched the complex plan to get him here.

'And why was that? Wasn't he wealthy enough?'

The deliberate insult was sheer, instinctive self-defence. The moment the words were said he regretted them deeply. His own wealth had never interested her during their marriage, and afterwards she'd returned every one of the generous monthly allowance cheques he'd had his solicitor send on his behalf.

To his eternal shame, he saw her slim shoulders shake with sobs, her pale hands covering her face. He abandoned his hard-won caution and pulled her into his arms. What he felt for this woman was far stronger than wisdom.

He loved her, moral warts and all. He had tried, God knew he'd tried, but he couldn't stop loving her.

'Don't cry. Please don't cry!' His voice was raw with emotion. He couldn't bear her to be hurt. He'd accused her of being something she never could be—a gold-digger, someone with her eye on the main chance. He knew that whatever else she was, she wasn't that. She had always been extraordinarily naive about financial matters. 'What I said was unforgivable,' he declared against her hair, gathering her closer.

Bella lifted her head from his shoulder to search his face, and the emotion coming from him bound them together in something sweeter than mere forgiveness. The anguish in his eyes was unmistakable. He rarely showed his emotions—she knew that—but when he did they were the genuine article.

The way he'd lashed out at her had torn her apart, but his remorse was cementing the pieces back together. She opened her mouth to accept his apology and heard him groan, his head dipping as his lips stopped the words in her throat.

His kiss was raw passion. Bella returned it—because this was what she'd been born for. To be his love, and only his. She had always loved him, always would. Like it or not, this man was her destiny.

The wild race of blood through her veins matched the burning fever of his as, bodies clinging, lips plundering and willingly plundered, they moved, dreamlike, into the tiny hall and Jake closed the door behind them with his foot.

'Bella—' he murmured, but she made a guttural

sound of protest and pulled his head down to hers again. She moved her mouth slowly, erotically, over his, tasting, stroking, melting under the onslaught of his wild response, her sweet seduction bringing his answering driven passion.

She curled her arms more tightly around his shoulders, wanting to stay where she belonged. In his arms. Under his skin.

In his life?

CHAPTER NINE

IT WAS the sweet breath of sanity at last, drawing them back to where they belonged. Together. As they were meant to be, as they'd been born to be—no longer apart, lost souls in an empty, cold, black void. Together.

Her bedroom. Bella didn't exactly know how they'd got there. It wasn't important. Only the hot hunger of Jake's mouth as he branded every inch of her body with his raw possession mattered.

Her flesh trembled, ached, burned for him. And her hands were making a clear, silent statement of fevered repossession as her fingers dug deeply, stroked and stroked again, exploring every millimetre of that strong, demanding male body. The body she knew so intimately—every muscle, every bone, every last pore of his sweat-slicked skin marked on her brain, never to be forgotten, not even if their parting had lasted through eternity. That was what was important, too. Nothing else.

Clothing scattered everywhere. Heated bodies close together, twisting, writhing in the immensity of their need to be closer still, so close that each was absorbed into the other. Fever and passion and the inescapable, beautiful simplicity of home-coming.

Bella arched her hips expressively, demandingly towards him, her whole body quivering. Her mouth was

urgently seeking his, tasting him, opening to the renewed savage plunder of his lips, responding fever-
ishly, drawing him into her, the invitation accepted by
him with a ragged groan as he slid deeply between
her parted thighs.

One moment of sheer, exquisite ecstasy. A still, un-
moving savouring of the rapturous, breathtaking moment of joining. Her body tightly enclosed his until
he gave a ferocious cry and plunged deeper, taking
them higher and higher into the wild storm of passion
until it took them both and shook them into a million
brilliant shards of pulsating light.

And then the slow descent to peace. Soft murmurs,
slow touching, the gentle glow of the aftermath—slick
bodies close, but softly now, her hair splayed out
across his firm, wide chest, her head fitting naturally
into the angle of his rangy shoulder and her lips moving softly against his hot skin. One of his hands idly
stroking the gentle flare of her hip, the other resting
heavily on the damp tangle of curls between her
thighs.

Bella sighed, a tiny fluttering exhalation, as peace
and tranquillity, both strangers for so long, took her
gently down to sleep.

The sky was black against the windowpanes but the
bedside light was on when she woke to the sound of
the door opening—Jake, naked, soft dark hair rumpled, carrying a tray.

'What time is it?' She raised herself up on one elbow, pushing her hair out of her drowsy eyes—
drowsy eyes drowning in love for him.

'Almost eleven. One more hour and it will be Christmas morning.' His lazy grin was heart-stopping. Bella actually felt her heart stop then start again, racing on out of control as he instructed gruffly, 'Move over, woman. I'm freezing. Warm me.'

She lifted the edge of the soft down duvet, her heart clenching with unadulterated joy as he slid his big body in beside her. Everything was right again; she knew it was. It just had to be!

Nothing had been said. Talk hadn't been necessary, after all. Their bodies had said everything that needed to be said.

Wrapping her arms around him, she cuddled her warm body against his icy skin, totally forgetting the loaded tray until Jake growled, 'Watch it! You want to share a bed with a mountain of toast and a lake of tea?'

The temptation to heave the tray off the bed and take her in his arms was enormous. They had made love in the very truest sense of the time-honoured phrase, and it had been all he had dreamed of during the last barren year. And more. So much more.

Yet there were questions he had to ask. Everything had seemed so cut and dried a year ago, almost to the hour, when he'd discovered her in her former lover's arms. The end. The love of a lifetime over and done with, shattered by what his eyes had told him.

But the events of the last couple of days, and the explosive need of the last hours, had shown him differently. It was far from over. Whatever happened it could never be completely over, not for him. Or for her?

He had to find out how much blame he carried for the way she'd taken up her old career, her old lover.

She was sitting up amongst the pillows, the pert, rosy tips of her breasts just visible above the edge of the duvet, her black hair a silken cloak around her slender white shoulders.

Jake said round the sudden constriction in his throat, 'Eat up. I woke starving, and didn't think either of us would want to cook at this time of night. My earlier efforts with sandwiches were enterprising, but scarcely edifying, so I played safe and made toast.'

'Looks scrummy.' Bella took a thick slice of hot buttered toast from the plate and bit into it enthusiastically, telling him round a mouthful, 'Your sandwiches were delicious, once I managed to get my mouth around them! Don't put yourself down. And I ate my share, or didn't you notice?'

He watched the tip of her tongue peep out, licking buttery fingers, and his heart clenched inside his chest. Of course he'd noticed. He noticed everything about her. Always had.

He took his mug of tea, cradling it in his hands, his voice carefully level as he asked, 'You mentioned that dream you had—about having a home in the country, a family. Did it mean so very much to you?'

She gave him a smiling, sideways look and helped herself to another slice of toast. She hadn't realised just how hungry she was. All the frantic, physical activity of a few hours ago, she thought, her cheeks going pink.

'It was what I'd always wanted,' she agreed. But it

didn't seem so important now. Jake's love, his trust, was all she craved. 'I suppose,' she added thoughtfully, 'the whole thing—a settled home, a loving family life—something I'd never had—took more room in my head than it should have done. Basically, I was lonely. You were away so much. Out of the three years of our marriage we spent one hundred and thirty-one days together. I kept a record. Does that make me paranoid?'

She supposed she must have been. She had counted days and hours, yearned for what she couldn't have, losing sight of what was truly important—that she loved him, no matter what.

'I had to be away, you knew that—or I thought you did,' he reminded her gently, his eyes soft as he watched how hungrily she devoured the toast.

He'd always known he had to stay ahead of the pack, not let anyone or anything pull him down. He had to be where the action was, use his brain, not rely on capricious luck as his father had done—losing everything in one fell swoop, plunging his loved ones into penury.

'You could have travelled with me,' he pointed out without rancour. If he'd known about her family background he would have understood the needs she'd had. It was important now for her to open up. And she seemed very relaxed right now, even smiling that wonderful, lazy smile of hers, the one that melted his bones right through to the core.

'I tried that, remember? Brussels, Rome, New York.' She took a gulp of tea. 'There was only so much window-shopping I could stomach, and the museums all began to look the same. I usually found myself having dinner alone in our suite because you were held up in meetings. And when you did get back you were toting loads of paperwork. So that kept you occupied until the small hours, and— Oh!'

Her hand hovered over the last slice of toast, withdrew. She picked up the plate and offered it to him guiltily. 'I've eaten the lot. I just wasn't thinking. Take this slice. I'm a greedy pig!'

'You want it, you eat it. I ate mine while I was making yours,' he fabricated. He would willingly starve rather than see her want for a single thing. Watching her eat with such unselfconscious enjoyment filled him with tenderness.

'So I gave up and decided I might as well stay home,' she completed. 'Not that it matters. Not now. Not at all.'

But it did. Jake knew it did. He knew now that he had his own burden of blame to carry. What had happened hadn't been all down to her. If they got this right—and he prayed to God that against all the odds they would—things would have to change. He was willing, if she was.

'And because you were bored you took up your modelling career again.' He could understand that now, though it had made him possessively jealous at the time. It had been her career, and one she had handled well.

He hadn't put any pressure on her, but had been deeply thankful when she'd abandoned it on their marriage. He had never been able to quell the unreasonable jealousy, the desire to make her his exclusive property, the overweening distaste at the thought of millions of nameless males lusting after her much-photographed face and body.

That, too, would have to change. If she wanted to pursue her career then that was what he wanted, too.

She twisted round in the cosy bed, and Jake moved imperceptibly away. He was aroused enough already. If she touched him there would be no more talk...

'You got it wrong,' she assured him, her lovely eyes shadowed. 'I've finished with modelling. You know that. When we married I told you I'd never stand in front of the cameras again. I meant it. Guy offered me the job of assistant manager in his agency's New Accounts department. So I took it. And I know we didn't need the money. My modelling career called on reserves of physical stamina, not the intellect, but I'm not a fool, Jake. I knew the healthy state of your bank balance, your investment portfolio.

'I knew all that.' She smiled into his eyes, not wanting to denigrate everything he'd given her, but knowing it was important to explain the way she'd felt. 'And, honestly, I knew our apartment was the last word in luxury—but you couldn't grow roses round the door or walk out barefooted onto dewy grass on a June morning. And there was a limit to the number of times I could change the decor, buy cushions and rugs and flowers.

'I guess—' her eyes mirrored her regret '—that by the time I decided to take that job as a way of occupying my time, we weren't heavily into communication. I told you I'd decided to accept Guy's job offer.

You assumed I'd be prancing in front of the cameras again.'

Not heavily into communication was an understatement, Jake accepted ruefully. During that last year of their marriage there'd been a total lack of anything remotely like togetherness.

He'd been increasingly aware of it at the time, putting it down to the large amounts of time he spent away from home. He had made up his mind to do something about it, had been on the point of telling her he'd delegate more, stay home, work from the London office. But it had been too late. He'd learned she'd been seeing Maclaine, had taken up her former career—or so he'd apparently wrongly assumed. He hadn't been able to handle that.

He removed the tray from where it lay on the bed between them and told himself it wasn't too late. He wouldn't let it be.

Already he had accepted the lion's share of the blame for what had happened. Bella had wanted, with more reason than most, the ordinary everyday things other people took for granted. A home that was a real home—not a sterile apartment that could have earned an award for being avant-garde—a husband who was around, babies. All the things he'd refused to give her.

The worst part would be coming to terms with her affair with Maclaine. The sudden insight hit him hard.

He didn't know whether he could handle it, learn to trust her again.

Bella watched as a shadow crossed his impressive features and took the light from his eyes. Her heart jerked. Had she complained too much when putting her point of view? But the air needed to be cleared if they were to go on. Were they to go on? And where to?

Had Jake made love to her simply because she was there? The sexual chemistry between them was as strong as ever; that was a fact of life and it wouldn't go away. Had her viewpoint of their marriage reinforced his conviction that they were poles apart in what they wanted, that all they had going for them was sex? Had he simply used her?

No, she thought decisively. Jake had far more integrity than that. And she was going to have to find a way to convince him that her dreams didn't matter. She'd woken up at last. The reality of loving him was the most important thing in her life.

'I'm going to take a shower.' She slid her long legs out of the bed, needing to lighten the atmosphere that had for some reason suddenly become brittle.

Perhaps her assumptions had been wrong, because the slow smile he gave her was warm enough to be reassuring. But he didn't follow her to share the shower, as she had more than half expected him to. When she emerged at last, clean and scented and unwrapping herself from a bath sheet, she thought he was asleep.

Eyes half-closed, she watched him. His male perfection made her breath stop in her throat. For all his muscular strength, his body was lean and elegant. He had fallen asleep on his back, his arms crossed behind his head, and Bella, suddenly, had never felt less like sleep in her life.

But she wouldn't wake him. She'd creep beneath

the duvet, cuddle up and stay awake all night, savouring every moment of this reconciliation.

Because it was a reconciliation, wasn't it?

Refusing to entertain negative thoughts, she selected a slinky, bias-cut satin nightie and wriggled into it. For the first time she thanked Evie for her meddling. Brushed cotton pyjamas wouldn't have had the same allure.

When he woke, Bella knew from delicious experience, Jake would make a slow, erotic game out of removing it. And it wouldn't be easy. A soft smile curved her mouth as she glanced down at herself. The oyster-coloured fabric clung to her breasts and tummy, then flared softly from just below her hips. Not a comfy garment to sleep in, but it made her feel good, supremely conscious of her femininity, her sensuality. She hadn't felt like that since she and Jake had broken up.

Her movements unconsciously sinuous, she walked towards the bed, her hand going out to snick off the bedside lamp, and Jake said, 'If you've finished, I'll use the bathroom.'

He sounded much too alert to have just this second woken. Why hadn't he spoken to her? Why had he kept his eyes so firmly closed? In the past, he had loved to watch her getting ready for bed, lazily teasing her, suggesting which of her huge selection of nightwear she should choose, then wickedly speculating on how long it would take him to remove it.

She almost switched the light back on so she could read his expression when she asked him. But she didn't do either. At this early stage of their reconciliation it might be too soon.

'Get some sleep, Bella.' His voice, she noted sinkingly, was distinctly abrasive. He vacated the bed as soon as she slid beneath the duvet. 'Watch the stars.' He sounded softer now, the suggestion light. 'It's a beautiful night, and if you listen hard enough you might just get to hear sleigh-bells!'

And then he was gone. Bella wanted to jump out of bed and run after him, but common sense stopped her. They'd been apart for a year, the break-up full of acrimony and distrust, their coming together again volcanic. He would need a little space to get things straight in his head, come to terms with the resumption of their marriage, let it sink in.

Just because she had no doubts at all it didn't mean he didn't have a few lingering around somewhere. So she'd give him that space and time. For as long as it took him to shower and come back to bed, anyway.

Then she'd wrap her arms around him and hold him close and tell him how much she loved him. How very much. Assure him that things would be different, that she wouldn't ask for what he couldn't give her. His love was all she needed.

Whenever he had to be away on business she'd go with him. Take a crash secretarial course, perhaps, kill two birds with one stone—feel useful and be useful.

Guy wouldn't be pleased when she quit on him. But he'd soon find someone to fill her post and, valued friend though Guy was, being with Jake was far more important.

Jake stood under the punishingly cold needles of the shower, his teeth gritted, his emotions in chaos. He'd never know how he'd kept his hands off her.

When she'd dropped the bath towel her skin, in the dim light, had gleamed like magnolia petals, the gentle, sensuous curves and planes of her body a voluptuary's dream.

He'd closed his eyes and kept them closed, fighting to quell the need—the need to make love to her until there was no space in his head for thought. But that would be morally wrong.

He loved her, and always would; that wasn't in doubt. And earlier their lovemaking had been spontaneous, inevitable. He grimaced, turning off the shower and reaching for a towel. He wouldn't touch her again until he knew he could take her back into his life without bitterness.

Until he came to terms with her affair, put it out of his head and learned to trust her again, there was no real way they could make a future together.

He was going to have to discover if that was possible.

He hoped to hell it was.

CHAPTER TEN

'YOU'RE up early,' Jake said.

Christmas morning, not yet quite light. And, yes, Bella was up early. She'd been up for ages. She was moving around the kitchen doing housewifey things to keep her mind from brooding over everything else.

'There's fresh coffee in the pot, and orange juice in the fridge. Help yourself while I cook breakfast.'

She sounded bright enough and normal, didn't she? She looked OK, clad in the faithful leggings and sweater, her hair neatly scooped back and fastened at the nape of her neck, the skilful application of make-up hiding the tell-tale signs of a miserable, wakeful night.

Just an ordinary woman doing ordinary things. Disguising the utter misery inside her, the hateful feeling of being used and discarded.

She laid bacon slices and tomato halves on the grill pan, then reached for the eggs, and Jake said, 'The full works, is it?'

He was leaning against the worktop sipping his juice, and her head came up as she caught the thread of tension in his voice. Dark sweater, dark jeans, shadowed black eyes. He had shaved, but he still looked as if he had a five o'clock shadow, the harsh lines of his face telling the story of his own restless night.

'As we're leaving tomorrow I thought we should use as much as we can from the fridge. Such a waste, otherwise.' She slid the bacon under the grill and drizzled some oil into the frying pan. Did she sound laid back and in charge of her life, all that inner despair and hopelessness nowhere in sight?

And what right did he have to look as if he'd spent last night tossing and turning, agonising, when she knew differently?

Waiting for him, all done up in slinky oyster satin, she'd snuggled into the blissful warmth of the duvet, watching the stars just as he'd suggested, rehearsing exactly how she'd tell him how much she loved him, how she'd changed her plans for the future so they'd fit happily with his. That he mustn't think she was making sacrifices because, when it came down to it, all she wanted was him.

She'd sort of mesmerised herself into falling asleep, waking in the early hours and not finding him beside her. Bewildered, disorientated and alone, she'd switched on the light and checked the time. Two o'clock. He couldn't have been in the shower for two whole hours!

Anxiety had taken over then. Had he slipped on the soap and knocked himself out? Leaping from the bed, she'd scurried to check. That vividly imagined disaster hadn't happened. But another one had. She'd discovered him sound asleep in his own bed.

He hadn't been lying awake, pretending, had he? She hadn't taken time to check. Just flicked the light on, viewed the rigid mound under the duvet that was similar to her own, and flicked it back off again. She'd crept back to her own room on leaden legs, saturated with that hateful, hurtful feeling of having been used.

He'd had no reason to pretend to be asleep. The facts punched holes in her brain. He hadn't wanted to be here, that was for sure. He'd even said their separation was a relief. He was a very physical man and she'd been around, and willing—more than—and was still his wife, of sorts. So he'd done what any man with rampaging male hormones would have done—taken advantage.

Used her and discarded her.

If he'd seen a future for them and their marriage he sure as hell wouldn't have gone back to his own bed! He would have come back to her, if only to talk, maybe suggest they try again, make a go of their marriage this time.

Suddenly aware that she was rapidly losing her precious control, rattling cutlery like castanets, practically hurling the china onto the table, and that Jake was watching her with narrowed eyes, she did her best to calm down.

She dragged in a deep and wobbly breath, and Jake took the knives and forks from her shaky hands.

'I'll see to the table; you keep an eye on the food.'

She turned away jerkily. She couldn't meet his eyes, not wanting to see cynical understanding or, even worse, lurking amusement.

Bacon was sizzling; eggs were popping and almost jumping around in the pan. She turned the heat down under them and rescued the bacon, making her movements smooth and contained now, forcing herself to keep calm because he was more than astute enough to read her mind, to laugh at her inside his head for being dumb enough to think that a couple of hours of mind-bending sex could alter anything.

He'd made the toast, and was dropping it into the rack when she slid the loaded plates down on the linen place-mats.

He held her chair out for her and she arranged herself in her seat, praying she looked relaxed enough to put him off the scent.

'Happy Christmas, Bella.' It sounded more like a question than a salutation. He joined her at the table. 'I don't have a gift for you, but you'll understand why, given the circumstances.'

Last year he'd chosen diamonds in New York. The only stones he knew that could come anywhere near the brilliance of her eyes.

The velvet-lined box had been in his breast pocket when he'd walked in the door and found her wrapped around Guy Maclaine.

He'd handed the gems over to charity.

'I could give you the perfume I'd brought along as a gift for Evie, only I don't quite see you ever using it,' she offered, the lightness of her tone achieved with enormous difficulty.

It was a silly, pointless conversation to be having, when the air they breathed was full of tension. Well, for her, at least. But she supposed the show had to go on—and all that stiff upper lip stuff. She picked up her cutlery and unconsciously emulated Jake, cutting her bacon into very small pieces and pushing them around her plate, unaware of his suddenly narrowed eyes focusing on her.

'You said Evie had meddled in your life before?' He gave up all pretence of eating and poured coffee for them both. Hot and strong and black, the way they both liked it. Could she have been telling the truth? Had she had nothing to do with this set-up at all?

Whoever had arranged it had done him a huge favour; he accepted that now. His hurt, the sense of bitter betrayal, had been too great to let him seek her out. Being forced into her company had allowed him to accept that he still loved her.

At first he'd disbelieved everything she'd said, colouring every word that came out of her mouth with the dark shades of that final betrayal. But he'd come to see that a lot of the blame for what had happened had been his, and he didn't want to believe that most of what she'd said to him was lies.

If he could get to the bottom of what had happened here it would be a start. She hadn't answered, was staring into space, apparently, cradling her cup in her long white hands. 'So what happened? What did she do?' He gave her a gentle verbal prod.

What did it matter? Bella gave an involuntary shrug and replaced her cup on its saucer. Still, she supposed the subject was unimportant enough—it certainly didn't have any bearing on what had happened between them last night—a subject he wouldn't want to have to discuss—and it would beat sitting around in silence.

And if last night hadn't meant a damn thing to him, had been simply a way of assuaging lust, then she could pretend it had been the same for her. Couldn't she?

'She entered a photograph of me for a nationwide competition to find what they called "the face of La Donna"—to launch the then-new exclusive range of cosmetics and fragrances. I didn't know a thing about it until I heard I'd won.'

She gave him a level look, hoping she was boring his socks off. The rags to riches storyline wouldn't mean a thing to him. As far as she knew he took the privilege of wealth for granted. All he'd ever wanted, in her experience, was more of it.

'At first I was embarrassed,' she remembered, 'then furious with her. A modelling career had never entered my head. But she was little more than a kid— only thirteen at the time—and we'd always been close, so I couldn't stay mad with her for long.'

'It must have changed your life.' He had always assumed she'd gone out for fame and fortune herself, capitalising on her fantastic looks. A slight frown indented his brow as he replenished their cups from the pot.

Had he assumed too much? If he'd been wrong about one thing, could he be wrong about others? Why hadn't he asked her more than the most basic questions about her earlier life? Because, to him, the past hadn't mattered. Only the present. He had won the only woman he'd ever truly wanted, and the time he'd spent with her had been filled with the wonder of the achievement, the wonder of her.

And the rest of the time—the majority of it, as she'd reminded him—he'd been bent on achieving success on success in the world of high finance. So what did that make him?

An over-achiever with no room in his head for the little things, the things that mattered. His self-esteem reached rock bottom.

'Dramatically,' she agreed, oblivious to his mental turmoil, gone away from him into the past. 'I was still in shock when I went for that first meeting with Guy. He was, and still is, of course, head of the agency which was running the launch campaign. I was painfully awkward, stiff and shy and terrified. He took me right under his wing,' she recalled, her mouth softening fondly. 'Guy made me see there was nothing to be frightened of and everything to go for. I honestly don't think I could have gone through with it without him.'

'Well, bully for him!' Everything inside him froze at her repeated and doting mention of that hated name. His reaction was instinctive, the bitterness of a man for his enemy.

Bella gave him a look of shock which quickly turned to angry, defensive castigation.

'He was the only person I could trust in those early days. He was my friend!' A true friend.

She gathered up the breakfast dishes with an angry clatter and dumped them on the drainer, her back to him as she snapped out, 'Without his monumental kindness I'd have backed out of the whole thing. Without his patience and expertise I would have frozen rigid the first time the cameras pointed in my direction!'

She turned the hot water on with a savage twist of her wrist. 'And I'd have missed out on the opportunity to give Mum an easier life, provide her with the things she'd never been able to afford to have.' She swiped their uneaten food into the wastebin. 'And because when Dad was with us we were always moving around Evie's education had been as patchy as mine. So we could then afford a private tutor for her, right? And first-rate secretarial training later. So I owe all that to Guy. Right?'

She was angry enough to do him physical damage. She skittered round on her heels and faced him. There had been no need for him to use that sarcastic tone. What had Guy Maclaine ever done to him? She had already countered his wretched suspicion of an affair between them. Or didn't he believe her?

The absence of trust had ended their marriage, but it hadn't ruined their reconciliation because there hadn't really been one. Just a cruel slaking of lust on his part and the obliteration of a stupid dream she'd had no right to indulge in on hers.

Or didn't trust really come into it as far as he was concerned? When he'd found her with Guy on that dreadful night, might it have been the escape route he'd been looking for? Had he grown tired of her? Bored?

She spat the new and hateful suspicions at him, her hurt at the way he'd used her love for him last night not letting her hold anything back. 'You want to believe I had an affair with Guy! It gave you the excuse you'd been looking for, didn't it? You never questioned what he was doing at our apartment that night, did you? You just called me a vile name and walked out!'

'If I'd stayed I wouldn't have trusted myself not to

wring both your necks!' He was on his feet now, black eyes slits, tormented by the memories of the thing he was trying so hard to come to terms with. 'I came back when I'd cooled down. You'd gone. Not to him, of course; he was still married. The note you left told me our marriage was over. I had to accept that—it made sense, after all.'

Bella stared at him, the pent-up emotions inside her making her shake. So little faith, and no trust at all.

She could have told him exactly why she'd been wrapped up in Guy's arms, but she wouldn't demean herself by offering explanations he wouldn't believe. Possibly because he wouldn't want to believe them.

'Believe what the hell you like—I'm beyond caring!' she ground out untruthfully, and, snatching her coat from the peg on the door, she walked out into the bright dawn of Christmas morning.

Jake forced back his instinct to go after her. She needed time to calm down. There was no doubt about it, he had a tigress on his hands.

There was a hidden emotional depth that he had never taken the time to plumb—that was going to change. If she'd agree to start over, he'd spend the rest of his life getting to know her. The real Bella, not just the fantastic face and body that had bewitched him from the moment he'd first seen her.

Keeping a watchful eye on her ferociously stamping progress up and down the cleared track, he methodically cleared up in the kitchen and lit a roaring fire. She'd come back inside when she'd got rid of all that fury.

And he'd treat her like spun glass, so gently, win her back to him.

The sensation of being at peace with himself at last flooded through him. He believed now that Evie had meddled with Bella's life in a big way for the second time, with the help of his own sister this time. But that didn't matter—or only inasmuch as he was back on course, trusting her not to lie to him.

What really mattered was the way he'd finally and suddenly come to terms with her infidelity.

He could easily understand how the affair had begun. Maclaine was attractive to women, and she'd been very young when he'd met her. And she'd been grateful to him for helping her to achieve the financial security she and her family had never known.

And later his own long absences, his dedication to his work, his thoughtless prevarication when she'd mentioned babies, telling her they'd discuss all that some time in the vague future, had eventually driven her back to her former lover—the man who, or so it now seemed, had given her one hundred per cent of his attention.

His shoulders were broad enough to carry all of the blame, and in the future—if she'd give them a future—he would provide her with everything she craved for. He'd sort that out as soon as they got away from here.

But until he could show her that his good intentions were more than the hot air and vague promises he'd carelessly tossed at her in the past, and could offer her the solid physical proof that everything had changed, he'd walk as if he were treading on eggs.

He wouldn't use their physical need for each other to blackmail her into being part of his life again.

The release from the canker of bitterness and anger was exhilarating. It had been nudged out of sight by the one great constant in his life—his love for her.

He crossed again to the window. Halfway down the track her slender body was dwarfed by the icy immensity of the snow-clad mountains. His heart surged with the determination to make their future as perfect as it could possibly be, keep her close to him, as much a part of his life as she was a part of his heart.

He prayed to God she'd give him a second chance.

When Bella walked back in, the scene was festive. Leaping firelight, sherry and two small tulip glasses side by side on the coffee-table, Jake fixing a strand of multicoloured fairy lights on the tree.

She felt as if she were on the outside looking in, a kid with her nose pressed to the window pane watching yearningly something it could never be part of.

'You forgot to use the lights.' Carefully Jake gave her the most casual glance, the smallest smile. He wouldn't give her so much as a nudge towards the decision he was determined she would make when he'd put his own life in order.

'I didn't know how to fix them.'

If he wanted innocuous conversation she'd give it to him. Right now she felt too weary to fight him. She'd walked the rage out of her system and, although it would probably come back—trailing hurt and the feeling of being used and discarded—she was too drained at the moment to cope with anything other than the superficial.

Jake crawled round the base of the tree and pushed the plug into the socket. 'There.' He stood up, veiled eyes on her face, watching the way her eyes widened as the brilliant little lights came on, all the colours of the rainbow strung along the forest-green branches of the tree.

Something caught at his heart and tipped it over. Until her success she'd probably never had her own Christmas tree. Her father wouldn't have wasted money on such a thing, and after he'd run out on them all her family had probably had a struggle even to afford to eat.

Their first Christmas together had been spent at that rambling, Elizabethan inn, the two subsequent ones in the sophisticated elegance of a Bahamian hotel. The third—the third had been an unmitigated disaster.

But from here on in things were going to change. A sudden mental picture of the two of them dressing an enormous tree, stacking brightly wrapped gifts around it, flashed into his mind. It was followed by the moving image of a bunch of children—their children—galloping down the stairs at first light to investigate what Santa had brought them.

The future as she had always wanted it to be was what he wanted, too. And it was what they were going to have.

'What should we do about that turkey?' he asked lightly. He wanted to take her in his arms and paint a picture of the future they would have together. But it was too soon. He had to tread gently, give her proof positive of his good intentions first.

'Oh.' Bella blinked, and the dancing lights stopped mesmerising her. 'Cook it and eat it, I suppose.' Could she pretend they were a normal couple spending a normal Christmas together?

It was, she supposed, the only civilised thing to do.

'Then we'll do it together.'

Bella flinched. His smile was so warm it hurt her. She nodded, walking into the kitchen ahead of him, taking off her coat as she went. He was an enigma.

Two hours ago they'd been almost at each others throats, the pain of the last year spilling out. And now he was behaving as if it hadn't happened. As if last night hadn't happened.

What had happened between them last night was something he'd already put behind him. He didn't want to talk about it, or think about it, and he certainly didn't want to repeat it. As far as he was concerned it had been a one-night stand.

She would have to dig deep to find the strength to cope.

CHAPTER ELEVEN

IT WAS almost a relief to be heading away from the cottage at last. She wouldn't let herself dwell on all the painful regrets.

Bella sneaked a look at Jake's strong profile, and then wished she hadn't. There was an aura of excitement about him that was positively tangible. If she touched him she'd probably get an electric shock.

The prospect of getting away and dumping her safely back at her flat, out of the way, getting on with his own highly successful life must have mega-appeal if it made him look like that. It was as if he simply couldn't wait!

'The mechanic they sent out was on the ball,' he commented as they left the valley behind them and turned carefully onto the mountain road, the surface of which was compacted with frozen snow, just as the valley track had been. 'With us at nine, on the dot. That's what I call service.'

Bella said nothing. What was there to say? His heart-felt, appreciative comment had only reinforced what she'd just been thinking about his eagerness to put her out of his life again.

He'd been ready and waiting when she'd come downstairs that morning at a few minutes before nine, champing at the bit, as she'd described his mood to herself. He must have been up for hours. Everywhere was clean and tidy—the hearth swept clear of ashes, the baubles and lights taken down from the tree and stowed neatly away in their box. And that, more than anything else, had made her feel as if her world had stopped.

It was as if the time they'd spent together hadn't happened. And when the rescue vehicle had come into sight, advancing slowly down the track, he'd been out of the door as if someone had sprung a trap.

She'd built up a foolish dream, founded on nothing more substantial than hope, and he'd stamped on it. And this morning's breathtaking eagerness to get back to his life was grinding her silly dream into the ground.

And it hurt!

'I must remember to arrange to have flowers sent to Evans' wife,' he murmured, concentrating minutely on his driving because the conditions were on the side of downright dangerous.

Because the driver of the tractor had been instrumental in arranging his escape, Bella deduced acidly. She wished he didn't feel he had to make idle conversation, as if she were a stranger he felt he had to entertain.

'I suppose,' she answered dully, too miserable to care, and Jake took his eyes from the road for a second, sweeping them over her tight features.

'Headache still bothering you?' he asked softly.

As if he cared! 'Not at all,' she disclaimed stiffly, and looked pointedly out of the window at her side. The headache was fictional. She'd made it up because she hadn't been able to stand another second of the false spirit of Christmas.

Yesterday, while the turkey had been roasting, they'd lunched on nuts and sherry, picked at a salad and a bowl of fresh fruit. And he'd followed her everywhere. Wherever she'd been he was there, at her shoulder. Helping. They'd prepared the vegetables together and he'd laid the table in the living room, unearthing candles from somewhere, so they'd dined by candlelight and firelight and the glitter from the tree.

Oh, she'd tried to be adult and civilised about it, but the tension had wound her up to the point of almost saying something she'd regret, coming out with something decidedly personal, like telling him she loved him so much she thought she was dying from it, and begging him to take her back!

She wouldn't have been able to bear his pity, contempt or plain disbelief when he thanked her for the offer but said he wouldn't take it up, if it was all the same with her. Because that was what would have happened; she knew it in her bones. Otherwise why had he brought the shutters down so effectively?

So she'd invented a headache, blamed it on too much wine, and gone to bed. Where she'd known she'd be safe. And so she had been. He hadn't so much as poked his head round the door to say goodnight.

She spent most of the seemingly interminable journey wishing it was over so she could crawl into her own space, be alone and lick her wounds. But when at last they drew up in front of the mews flat she shared with Evie, Bella panicked. He was her husband, and she'd probably never see him again. If the past year was anything to go on he'd avoid her like the plague.

She simply couldn't go on like this.

He cut the engine and turned to her, and she got in first, before he could say anything—anything at all. 'We never did get around to discussing the divorce.' And she watched his face go tight.

'Divorce isn't in the frame,' he ground out through his teeth.

Was that anger in his black, black eyes? Or shock? Bella didn't know, or care. It was enough to have brought it home to him that she did exist, as his wife, albeit estranged. That she wasn't a passing stranger he had decided to be polite to, to the extent of making general, idle conversation to while away the time.

If he didn't like to be reminded that they were still legally tied, then tough! She would force the situation down his throat if she had to.

Ever since they'd made love he'd brought the shutters down. He treated her with politeness, with impersonal consideration, like a stranger. It was far harder to bear than when he'd been openly scathing, angry with her and at the situation they'd been put in.

'Why not?' she countered, her voice splintering with anger. She'd get a real response from him if it killed her! 'Our marriage is over, despite the mutually satisfying romp we had on the night of our fourth wedding anniversary.'

She'd stress that, oh, she would! He'd hurt her too much. The need to retaliate in kind was despicable, she knew that, but she hadn't been able to stop the raging words from falling off her tongue.

'You don't know what you're saying,' he told her. His face was white beneath the olive tones of his skin.

So she had forced a reaction, even if it was merely anger at her temerity in daring to mention something he had probably already conveniently forgotten.

'Oh, but I do,' she answered him back. 'Despite the sex, which I have to admit was well up to standard, our marriage was over the moment I knew you didn't trust me. I knew you didn't love me because, the way I see it, trust has to be the biggest part of loving. You immediately thought the worst, and went on thinking it. And believing it. I knew then that there wasn't any point.'

He wasn't answering. He looked as if she had just exploded a bomb under him. 'If you don't want to discuss divorce, we'll forget it,' she conceded finally, flatly, the fight draining from her, leaving her feeling weak and hopeless.

Divorce wasn't in any way important to her. It wasn't as if she would ever want to remarry. Jake was the only man she had ever loved, could ever love. She'd only mentioned it to get a real response.

She could see his point of view, too. Despite her having returned every one of the allowance cheques that had come through his solicitor, he might be understandably wary of the final break.

A divorce settlement could cost him heavily. The acquisition of wealth seemed the only thing that mattered to him. He wasn't to know she would never accept a penny from him, and he might suspect she would take him for all she could get, simply out of spite, if the break was made final.

'Bella—' He shifted in his seat, facing her now. He took one of her hands in both of his, and she let it stay there. It was beyond her power to snatch it away, and she self-destructively impressed this final touch on her memory banks. 'We do need to talk. Make arrangements for the future. At the cottage—' impressive shoulders lifted heavily '—the time wasn't right. You said trust was important.'

His eyes seemed to be probing her soul. 'I'm working on it, believe me. And I'm asking you to trust me now. We'll meet soon, have dinner, sort everything out.' The look in his eyes told her he wanted that very much.

Stupid hope soared again, filling her heart until she felt it might burst, and try as she might she couldn't stop it.

'When?' she asked, her voice low and husky, hoping he'd suggest the very next day.

'Soon,' he promised vaguely, his eyes hooded now as he rubbed his thumbs over her knuckles lightly before releasing her hand. 'I'll be in touch. I can't say when. I've a fair amount of business to attend to.'

So what else was new?

She released her seat belt, the momentary insanity of hope draining away. Business would always take precedence. Didn't she already know that? She scrambled out onto the slushy pavement. He would have far more important things to do than wine and dine his estranged wife, to talk her into accepting the status quo.

Because that was what it was all about. She was sure of that now—keep everything the same, a wife, but no wife, tucked away, never seen, making no demands. Avoid having to swallow a divorce settlement that would make a dent in all that money!

'I'll see you when I see you, then.' Echoes of the past! Of the times when she'd watched him walk out of the apartment, immaculately suited, briefcase in hand, his thoughts already gone from her, on another plane entirely. And had that been her voice, all high and hard?

She slammed the passenger door, lifted her bags and walked away, knowing she wouldn't see him again—because when he did get round to finding the time to make that date she'd tell him to get his solicitor to put whatever was on his mind in writing!

No way would she put herself through the hell of seeing him again.

For the rest of that day and the whole of the next Bella was alone. No sign of Evie. She felt more isolated than she'd been at the cottage. At least she'd had Jake for company.

But she wouldn't think about Jake, she vowed. Not ever again. Yet when the phone rang, startling in the silence, her stomach churned over sickeningly. Jake? Making that dinner date? Making time for her in his busy, busy life?

It was her mother, phoning long distance.

'I tried to get you on Christmas Day. Both out enjoying yourselves, were you?' She didn't wait for a reply. 'Your auntie sends her love. She's thinking of coming back with me when I visit again in the summer. You won't mind? Is Evie in? Is she still seeing that Mitchell boy? He's something in computers, isn't he?'

A sudden change of tone told Bella that she was about to come out with what had been uppermost in her mind. 'Have you and Jake got together yet and tried to sort things out?'

Bella ignored that for the moment. She'd answer briefly and in context. 'Evie's not here. She found out Bob Mitchell was already married and dropped him. At the moment I think she's got a crush on her new boss, so she's bounced back, as usual. And Jake and I have nothing to sort out. Our marriage is over. And my job's keeping me—'

Her mother wasn't interested in her job. 'Both you and Jake need a spanking!' she cut in. 'You're two lovely people, you had a lovely marriage. So you had a tiff, a difference of opinion—that's not the end of the world. All couples have them—'

Bella switched off. 'A difference of opinion' was putting it too mildly. They had both wanted vastly different things. But she had been willing to change, to want what he wanted, because she'd wanted to be back in his life. She'd been sure she could learn to live with his lack of trust; surely she could if she really tried? It was a flaw in his character she could do nothing about.

She would have told him, tried to pull their marriage back together, but he'd withdrawn the intimacy that would have made it possible. And now she was thankful she hadn't set herself up for the unbearable humiliation of having him tell her he wasn't interested.

'So it isn't any wonder, is it? Bella?'

'Sorry, Mum, I didn't quite catch that.'

'That I worry about you.'

'Then don't. I'm fine, really I am. Getting on with my life, making friends.' She gently steered the conversation away from the subject. Her mother had had a dreadful marriage and, understandably, she wanted her daughters to fare better. Bella couldn't blame her for nagging, but when the call ended she knew she had to do what she'd said—get on with her life.

She had her job and she enjoyed it. And she had the new friends she'd made at the agency. In the past, when she'd been invited to socialise, she'd always politely refused. Not any more. She would start to do some inviting of her own.

She picked up the phone. She'd call Guy and Ruth first, find out if the New Year party they were throwing at their home, with agency staff welcome, was still on. If it was she'd invite herself.

She heard the key in the lock as she ended the call. Evie. Anger at what her sister had done came back with a blistering whoosh.

Wearing a blue silk shift that matched the colour of her eyes and clung to her curvily plump figure as if it had been grafted on, Evie swayed on her very high heels and croaked, 'What are you doing here?'

'Waiting for you. Wondering which floorboard to bury your body under!'

'Oh, don't!' Evie looked as if she was about to burst into tears. 'Don't shout. I'm dead on my feet! I went to a party on Christmas night and it went on and on. I'm *still* recovering from it—I've got this splitting head!'

'Good.'

'And I'm freezing cold. I lost my coat—or someone stole it. I swear I'll never go to another of Lizanne's parties again as long as I live!'

'For an adult woman with a new boss and responsible job you certainly know how to act like a cretin!' Bella snapped. The Christmas conspiracy involving her and Jake and the type of irresponsible adolescent party that went on for forty-eight hours coalesced into one huge, unforgivable whole.

Then, seeing the tears trickle down the pale, pretty face, Bella relented. The mention of her job, the new boss Evie rarely stopped talking about, was probably responsible for the overflow.

Sisterly feeling prompted her to offer, 'Take those ridiculous shoes off and go and sit down. I'll make a pot of black coffee.'

All her life, or so it seemed, she'd been caring for Evie. She could vividly recall the two of them snuggling down in bed, the blankets pulled up over their heads to muffle out the sound of their parents shouting at each other, and Bella telling stories to take her little sister's mind off what was going on.

And later, after their father had gone, she'd had to take full responsibility for the bouncy, irrepressible Evie because their mother had had to be out at work to keep them.

So she'd learned responsibility early; it was only a pity some of it hadn't rubbed off on her sibling!

'What you and Kitty did was inexcusable,' she stated now, her clear eyes condemning. Strong black coffee and the warmth of the central heating had worked wonders; Evie looked almost like her old, bouncy self. 'You had no right to interfere in my life—or Jake's, for that matter!'

Evie curled herself more closely into the back of the armchair, pulling the cushion from behind her and wrapping her arms around it as if for protection against sisterly wrath.

'It was the only thing we could think of,' she defended. 'You're both obviously still crazy about each other, but refused to get together and thrash things out. Too much pride,' she tacked on scornfully. 'So Kitty and I worked out the scam last October—to force you to meet and stay together for at least a couple of days. We thought it was time enough for you to get your act together, anyway.'

Bella, pacing the room, swivelled round and glared. 'My only consolation is that the "scam", as you call it, will have cost you both a mini fortune!'

'I guess you're telling me it didn't work,' Evie said mournfully. 'We only did it for the best. Cos we love you, even if you are both stupid! Think about the mess our parents made of their marriage and compare it with what you and Jake had.' Her voice wobbled. 'What you had was beautiful. It used to be a joy to see you together.'

Bella stopped mid-pace, her justifiable annoyance over Evie's meddling washed away by a flood of tears that brimmed her eyes and clogged her throat. The two younger sisters had been desperate to help. But all the beauty had gone out of the marriage that had started so perfectly. Nothing could make it come back.

She swallowed hard and made herself go and perch on the arm of Evie's chair. 'You're going to have to accept that it's over,' she said quietly. 'I have. And no amount of good-intentioned meddling will alter that.'

Evie lifted a troubled face. 'Did you explain about that Maclaine chap? Tell Jake it wasn't what he thought it was?'

'Yes. I told him Guy had never been my lover.'

'And?'

Bella shrugged expressively. She'd told him the truth, but she didn't know now whether he'd believed her. How could trust be so easily shattered?

'After he'd got over his anger at the way we'd been tricked he behaved reasonably and considerately.' She wouldn't confess to the way they'd made love. She couldn't. It had happened because she still loved him and he still lusted after her. The sexual chemistry between them was still as explosive as ever. But it wasn't enough for either of them.

'Then, when he dropped me off here on Boxing Day, he would have driven away with nothing more than a polite goodbye. But I mentioned divorce, to remind him we were still married. But he doesn't want one. Too costly, I would imagine.'

Her voice hardened. 'He wouldn't want a dent in his precious fortune.' She pushed herself on, knowing she had to forestall any questions before she could draw a line beneath the traumatic episode. 'He then decided he'd better give me dinner some time—fit it in when he had a convenient space in his work schedule—to persuade me that this separation should continue as it is, in his own best interests.'

'Oh, Bel, don't be so cynical! It's not like you.'

'Just looking at life through untinted specs.' Bella pushed herself to her feet. She couldn't talk about it any more, relive the pain in words that skimmed the surface of the truth and left out the emotions that wouldn't go away. 'I'll forget what you did on the condition it's never mentioned again. And now I think it's time we both turned in.'

Bella had dug deep in the back of her wardrobe and found the perfect dress for the party. Shimmering gold tissue, scoop-necked and clingy—displaying too much leg maybe, but why the heck not? If you've got it, flaunt it, as her model friends would have said!

Anyway, it was New Year's Eve, and she was going to have fun. Yes, she was, she told the annoyingly sad eyes that stared back at her from her bedroom mirror.

Ruth, Guy's wife, had said, 'Oh, yes, do come, Bella. The more the merrier, truly! Most of the agency staff are going to be putting in an appearance at some stage, not to mention a load of mine and Guy's friends. I just hope the noise won't disturb the twins. But Mother-in-law came up from Sussex for Christmas, and she's still here. So she'll be on hand if they do wake. She's an old battleaxe, but she's really good with the babies.'

So she would socialise for a change. Besides, Jake

hadn't contacted her. She hadn't really expected him to, had she? Giving her dinner, talking over the arrangements for their separate future would come very low down on his list of priorities.

Everyone else would be taking a break over the festive season, but he would be jetting to wherever the next killing could be made, poring over balance sheets and financial projections.

She caught her thoughts and slapped them down brutally. She'd made an early New Year resolution never to think of him again. She was going to stick to it!

Starting the fiddly business of piling her hair on top of her head, she thought about Guy and Ruth instead. They had moved to a big family house in Hampstead before the birth of the twins. She was truly happy for them, and wasn't going to fall into the trap of envy.

They'd had a rough ride. A year into the La Donna campaign Guy—her dear friend by then, and professional support—had confided that he and Ruth were having a trial separation. They were finding it difficult to be around each other, he had told her.

'Ruth's desperate to have kids, but nothing happens. We've had every test known to medical science and we're both OK. So she blames me for not caring either way, and herself for caring too much. She can't leave it alone. She's getting paranoid and I'm getting irritable. Next thing, she'll be blaming the government, or the weather! We thought we'd be better apart for a while, before we start throwing things at each other.'

But things had worked out for them in the end.

When Guy had phoned on Christmas Eve, over a year ago—

No. No. No! She must not, *would* not think of any of that!

'Your taxi's here.' Evie poked her dark curly head round the bedroom door. 'Are you ready, or shall I ask him to wait?'

'Ready.' Bella pushed the final pin into her hair and stood up, reaching for her wrap and the gold kid evening purse that went with the dress. 'Are you sure you don't mind being on your own? You could come with me. One more won't make any difference.'

Evie shook her head decisively. 'After Lizanne's thrash I'm off parties.' Her blue eyes went dreamy. 'I thought I'd check through my wardrobe to find something suitable but less stuffy to wear for work. Maybe try out a new hairstyle.'

The new boss, Bella thought, turning away quickly and descending the stairs as rapidly as she could in high, spindly heels.

She could hardly bear to see the glow in the younger girl's eyes.

She could remember exactly what it felt like to fall in love.

CHAPTER TWELVE

HE WOULD be gatecrashing, but Jake didn't give a damn!

When he'd phoned from his hotel near Regent's Park he'd got Evie. He'd missed Bella by about half an hour.

Evie had started to apologise for tricking him, and putting his hired car out of commission, but he'd cut her short. After that getting information on Bella's whereabouts had been like pulling hen's teeth.

The information had come reluctantly. She didn't know when her sister would be back. Late, probably. It was New Year's Eve.

She had gone to a party.

A party in Hampstead.

And—this came most reluctantly of all—a party at the home of Guy and Ruth Maclaine.

The address had had to be forced out of her, and then she'd gone on to say something else, something rushed and breathless which he had cut short, telling her thanks and goodbye.

When he'd put down the receiver his heart had been pounding, the hatefully familiar shaft of jealousy which he'd believed he had conquered twisting his gut.

But he wouldn't let all that concentrated hard work go to waste. Not without a bloody hard fight.

He'd spent the last five days on the phone, setting up meetings and dragging people from family celebrations, pulling rank and generally making himself unpopular, fitting in a flight to Brussels, where he'd worked into the small hours consolidating deals, and then back to London to appoint key personnel.

He hadn't borrowed precious time from other people's family Christmases and worked himself to the point where exhaustion felt like a distinct possibility to get stymied at this last moment—particularly not by his own possessive streak where Bella alone was concerned.

He pushed any unwelcome doubts roughly aside and strode through the foyer, past the elaborately uniformed doorman, into the flurries of sleet that came on the back of a biting wind.

He didn't notice the cold or the damp flakes of wet snow that settled on the shoulders of his dark-grey suit jacket and drifted amongst the soft strands of his black hair, or the glittering Christmas decorations strung overhead as he flagged down a cruising taxi and gave the Hampstead address in a hard, tight voice.

Back at the cottage, when she'd told him Maclaine had never been her lover, he hadn't believed her. He had believed what his old friend Alex had said all those years ago because he had no reason not to. But, more importantly, he had believed the evidence of his own eyes.

Mercifully, he'd come to terms with it. He'd made too many wrong assumptions in the past—about Bella's resumption of her modelling career, the set-up back at the holiday cottage. Had he been wrong to assume she'd been unfaithful? Could what he had seen that dreadful night have a perfectly innocent explanation?

He didn't know, not for sure. How could he?

He pushed that thought roughly aside. He had to build on the future and not brood negatively on the past.

When she'd talked to him of trust, and his lack of it within their marriage, sincerity had been exhaled with every breath, had shone steadfastly in those fantastic eyes.

Against all the evidence he had instinctively accepted her innocence. What he had seen could be explained away. He had to believe that. He only had to ask.

He remembered his decision not to ask her there and then to resume their marriage, not to plead with her. And wondered for the first time if it had been the right one to make. Self-doubt was a stranger to him, though, and he knew what he wanted. Knew that what he wanted would be the right thing to do.

When he gave her the gift of the rest of his life, his entire future, his complete and infinitely loving attention, he wanted it to be whole, accomplished, not vague promises which—and with hindsight he couldn't blame her—she very probably wouldn't take seriously.

That was what he had now—the gift of his total commitment. He prayed to God it wasn't too late.

When she'd mentioned divorce, spoken so tonelessly of that mutual eruption of need—the wild desire, the fulfilment they'd both ached for twelve long months—the temptation to take her in his arms, kiss her until she was unable to think of anything but him, had been almost unbearable.

But he'd stuck to his original decision, and all he had been able to do was promise to contact her as soon as he was able, ask her to give him what he'd been unable to give her. Trust.

But what if he'd been wrong? Had she decided that an affair with Maclaine was the better option?

If rumour was correct, the Maclaine marriage had been on the rocks. But they were obviously together now. Was that a so-called civilised arrangement? Was Maclaine presenting a façade of a contented marriage but unable to let go of his creation—the exquisitely beautiful face and body of La Donna?

And was Bella clinging to him because he was a constant in her life? Her father sure as hell hadn't been, and he, although he hadn't realised it at the time, hadn't been much better.

He closed his eyes, his teeth clamped together. He would not let himself think like that. He would not doubt her. Not again. He would not!

The taxi pulled up outside the large Edwardian house. Lights blazed from the lower-floor windows, and security spotlights illuminated a sweeping driveway packed with parked cars.

Asking the driver to wait, Jake strode towards the house, unaware that the sleet had turned to heavy rain, soaking him, plastering his hair to his skull.

Bella wished she hadn't come, and tried to hide it. Her first attempt at socialising wasn't bringing her any pleasure—far from it.

Maybe it was simply down to the time of year. The Christmas season was for sharing with loved ones. Everyone here was part of a couple, and the crunch had come when she'd overheard one woman saying to another, 'Getting babysitters at this time of year is almost impossible. And New Year's Eve—we had to pay an absolute fortune!'

And her companion had confided, rubbing her slightly bulging tummy, 'My dear, John and I will be in the same boat this time next year. Oh, lovely thought! We're both ecstatic at the prospect of starting a family.'

Bella had wished herself a million miles away, because everything reminded her of what she wanted and couldn't have.

Jake. Jake's love. Jake's babies.

Bella's fingers tightened round her wineglass. She'd drunk half of it, but it hadn't helped get her in the party mood, and Ruth said concernedly, 'Are you all right? You went quite pale just then.'

'I'm fine.' Bella managed a creditable smile. 'A bit tired, that's all.'

'Hectic Christmas?'

'You could say!' Traumatic, devastating, ecstatic and truly, truly painful. Did that add up to 'hectic'? She wondered how she could still be smiling. The smile was stuck to her face, she supposed.

Ruth said, raising her voice because the noise level was continually increasing, 'I'm going to slip away and check on the twins and Ma-in-law. Would you like to see them?'

'I—' Bella didn't see a way to get out of this. But gazing at four-month-old baby boys didn't seem a good idea right now, not when she was feeling so vulnerable.

Then Guy came to her rescue, catching the tail-end of the conversation, throwing an affectionate arm around Ruth's shoulders.

'Bella can gaze in wonder at my handsome twin heirs later. Right now I've a business proposition to put to the lady.'

'Oh— You!' Ruth twisted in his arms and reached up to brush her knuckles playfully over his rock-solid chin. 'Business, business! Give the girl a break—she's come to a party, not a strategy meeting, or whatever!' Nevertheless, she went, wagging her fingers at Bella. 'See you later. If you want to party, tell him to get lost!'

But Bella heaved a sigh of relief at the timely interruption. She had never felt less like partying in her life, and, though normally she would have loved to slope away and peek at the little boys, she knew it would be her undoing. Tears and abject misery for all she had lost and could never now have would have made her the party-pooper from hell!

'Listen...' Guy took her arm and drew her to a marginally quieter corner of the big room, away from the lavish buffet. 'I've been thinking of you. We had a big—and I mean big—commission confirmed just before Christmas. In New Accounts you'll know all about it—the new top-of-the-range sports car, aimed primarily at top-of-the-range females?'

Bella nodded; she knew all about the prestigious account. Her immediate superior had worked his socks off to clinch it. A smile tugged at the corners of her mouth as Guy's bushy eyebrows met over the bridge of his crooked nose—broken on the rugby field, so Ruth had told her—his head tipped to one side as he peered down into her face.

He was her boss, and if he wanted to talk shop she was more than game. Her job was all she had now.

'I want you on it—not on the account; I can replace you in that department without too much trouble. But on film. As you know, the company want a series of six commercials running through spring and summer. I can't think of anyone who'd be as perfect as you. Will you do it? For me?'

His smile took her acceptance for granted, and it lit up his near-ugly face, making it wickedly attractive. Bella couldn't help responding in kind, but she knew she'd never go back to her former career. She had grown to hate all those greedy eyes, the endless speculation, the cruel, gossiping tongues.

She shook her head, reminding him, 'I've been out of it for too long. Four years, remember.'

'Nonsense.' He took her chin between his thumb and forefinger, eyes intently assessing every detail of her face. 'You're as beautiful as when you started out. More. You've acquired the gloss, the sophistication our clients want. You're one classy lady, Bella, and there's not a sag, wrinkle or line in sight!'

Her chin still captured in his hand, she gave him a

wistful smile. She would do a lot for Guy, but not this. Right through her earlier career he had been her rock, her very good friend. He had always been there for her when it had mattered, and, although only around fifteen years her senior, she had come to look on him as a father-figure.

'I'm sorry,' she whispered regretfully. 'But I'm happy as a pen-pusher. I couldn't go back to all that hype and frenzy—flashbulbs exploding wherever I go, spiteful gossip in the press, endless speculation.' She gave him an impish grin. 'I only did it because we were flat broke, and the money meant Mum could take it easy and Evie could realise her full potential and not end up as another unemployment statistic. You know that!'

She saw the light go out of his eyes, and knew he'd had the campaign sorted in his head, with her in the starring role. She felt a tug of compassion. Lifting a hand, she laid it softly on the side of his craggy face. 'With your talent for picking winners, you'll find the perfect girl, I promise. There are literally hundreds of young and beautiful models out there, waiting for the opportunity you can offer. Go out and find that special one, Guy, and leave me pushing my pen.'

Standing in the open doorway, Jake felt his eyes home in on her immediately. He didn't see the crowd, the groups of chattering, laughing people. Only Bella and Maclaine.

The sensation of *déjà vu* was intense, jealousy, pain and the feeling of betrayal taking him by the throat, shaking him. Just as it had done on the night of Christmas Eve over a year ago.

As when he'd first seen her, at the party Alex had dragged him to she was the focus of all his attention, all his needs and desires. A raven-haired beauty in a shimmering dress. Maclaine was cupping her delicate face in his big paw, and she was, as before, curving her slender body into the support of his.

She was listening to what he was saying intently, her fascinating eyes locked with his, smiling a little now. And as Jake, in this crowded, over-heated room, saw only the two of them, so they, obviously, saw only each other.

His eyes closed as a pain so savage he thought it might rip him apart rocked him back on his heels. And when he forced them open again he saw her reach out a pale, slender hand and place it lovingly on the side of his goddamn ugly face.

And he knew he had lost her. For one moment, as his head bowed and his body sagged against the door-frame, he accepted his loss, and his world became a dark, empty, bleak place, a place he didn't want to be.

But only for a moment. He wouldn't jump to con-clusions. And he knew with a wild lifting of his heart that he trusted her. The scars had healed. Where he loved, he could trust.

Unaware of the curious eyes now turned to him, the gradual silencing of party-time chatter, he lifted his head, straightened his shoulders and pushed his way through the crowded room, his face, though grey with fatigue, scored with the arrogance of his determination.

The changing, charged atmosphere must have penetrated even their mutual absorption, he noted grimly as she turned and met the savage single-mindedness of his narrowed black eyes.

What colour she did have drained from her lovely face and then quickly returned, concentrated in two hectic splashes lying against the high perfection of her cheekbones.

He reached out, his fingers curling around her arm, just above her elbow, keeping himself under tight control because he couldn't bear to bruise that tender flesh. He would never do her even the slightest harm.

'What the hell do you think you're doing?'

Maclaine didn't recognise him at first; Jake could see it in his eyes. Then why should he? He hadn't gone out of the way to seek his former enemy's company. And he guessed the violence of his emotions must be stamped all over his face. Little wonder the man looked as if he was squaring up to throw him out of his house!

Jake left him in no doubt as to his identity, telling him smoothly, 'I've come to collect my wife. Lovely party, but I'm afraid we can't stay.'

Bella went with him without a murmur. She was shaking inside, but wouldn't let it show. Aware of the intense silence in the room, the murmurs that were beginning to break out in their wake, the politely muffled hum of excitement, she stared steadily ahead, every nerve in her body stinging in sharp response to the determined man at her side.

She didn't bother to find her wrap, didn't even think of it, wasn't aware of the lack of it until the cold wind, the deluge of rain, made her gasp.

Silently, he swept her into his arms and strode rapidly between the parked cars. His body was as taut as steel. Anger? Her shocked mind hopelessly grappled for reasons.

There was a black cab waiting at the kerb, the meter ticking over. Jake put Bella in the back and went to give the driver instructions, giving her the opportunity to get her head together.

His behaviour could only mean one thing—he still believed she and Guy were having an affair.

Could all that inner tension stem from the fact that she was still nominally his wife, his property, albeit unwanted property?

She couldn't believe that. He was the most urbane, controlled man she had ever known. It had to be something more, and yet she couldn't allow herself to hope. If he still loved her, needed her in his life, he would have told her so.

Wouldn't he?

'There was no need to act like a caveman,' she said in a rough little voice she didn't recognise as her own as he joined her and the cab drew away from the kerb. 'I would have left if you'd asked me in the normal manner. And you could have stayed, had a drink, joined in our conversation.'

She was plucking nervously at the hem of her dress. The fabric was sodden, even though he'd whisked her through the deluge as quickly as possible. And his clothes were worse, his hair plastered to his head.

In the dim interior light she could see the harsh black glitter of his eyes. He was having trouble hanging onto his precarious control; she knew that. The way his voice shook told her that. And one more push could do the trick, make him lose the last, tenuous hold and tell her exactly what this was all about.

She thought she knew—she hoped she'd got it right—but she needed to hear it from him.

Taking her courage in both hands, reminding herself that it was probably now or never, she said tartly, 'You still think I'm capable of having an affair with Guy, right under Ruth's nose! Is that what you think of me? And now you'll never know—were we whispering sweet nothings, counting the minutes until we could be properly alone? Or were we having a nice, friendly, innocent conversation? Tough, isn't it?'

She got a response. Not the one she'd expected. But the way he gave a smothered groan and dragged her into his arms told her all she wanted to know.

Jake felt her body tremble in fevered response, her arms going out to him, fingers tangled in his hair, holding his head to deepen the already fathomless kiss.

His mouth moved slowly over hers, tasting the sweet moistness of her lips. His hands stroked over her body, needing to touch all of her, feel the heady warmth of her flesh beneath the clinging damp cloth.

She still wanted him physically; he knew that. Nothing she could ever say or do could hide that from him. Not when he touched her. And that was all he ever had to do. She couldn't hide the fire and the fury, the sheer meltdown of her response.

It was something to build on, something no other man could ever take from him. All he had to do was convince her that his scars had healed, that he could trust her, could be there for her always if she still wanted him to be. All she had to do was say yes.

Becoming aware that the taxi was at a standstill, Jake lifted his head and almost drowned in the shine of her luminous, bewitching eyes.

'Where are we?' she murmured dizzily, hating the necessary withdrawal. In his arms there were no doubts, no fears. Together, close, they were one being, elemental.

'My hotel.' He helped her out. His voice was ragged. The doorman hurried down, holding a huge striped umbrella over them both. Bella felt certainty, the joy of coming home, swell up in her heart, spilling over in a smile that would not go away, and was still there, hovering on her mouth, when they reached his suite.

But his eyes were serious, his mouth tight. 'Get out of those wet things. Shower. I'll ring room service and get into dry clothes. After that, I've something to say to you.'

She shook her head and felt her hair finally tumble down, cloaking her shoulders. She pushed it back from her face impatiently. She wanted to get the talking over now. Stop him hurting. Tell him what she should have told him over a year ago.

If he didn't trust her as far as he could throw her, did it really matter? What right had she to expect him to be perfect? And would she have trusted him, in a similar situation?

A year ago she'd been rigid with pride. Now she had none where he was concerned. She stretched out her hands to him. 'Say it now. Please.'

'Later.' He ignored the offer to take her hands in his. His face could have been carved from stone. 'You're wet and cold. Do as I asked.' He tipped his head. 'The bathroom's through there.'

Dictatorial devil! she thought, but did as she was told because it seemed the quickest way to hear what he wanted to say to her. That he had decided to end the marriage, whatever the cost, seemed a distinct possibility. And yet the way he had claimed her, frog-marched her away from Guy and the party, the way he'd kissed her, his earthy moans of triumph when she had kissed him back...

Quivering with the tension of not knowing, she stripped off her sodden clothes and left them in a heap on the marble tiled floor. She felt as if she'd been wired up to an electric charge and any moment now would explode in a million fizzing sparks.

Her time under the shower was the absolute minimum, and she wrapped herself in the towelling robe supplied by the hotel management. All that done in record time, she suddenly quailed at the thought of going out there and hearing what he had to say.

She felt like a prisoner in the dock, waiting for the jury's verdict!

Grabbing a towel, roughly drying her hair, she felt armoured enough to face him. An attitude of casual insouciance would surely help her cope, hide the state of her nerves.

But the room was empty. And there was nothing in

the room to offer her any comfort. Luxurious, but impersonal. No sign of his occupation. She wondered how long he'd been staying here. Did he base himself here when he was working from London? She knew he'd off-loaded the Docklands apartment.

Didn't he ever feel the need for a home? A real, lived-in family home, where he could relax, let the rest of the world go hang, secure in his own personalised space?

Or didn't his surroundings matter to him? Was the acquisition of wealth and power the only truly important thing in his life?

And did surroundings matter to her? The answer, she knew, was yes. But he mattered more. She would live in a shoe-box with him, if he'd let her.

Room service had already delivered a tray of coffee. She wondered whether to pour herself a cup, but was afraid she wouldn't manage it. Her hands were shaking too much.

She let the towel slide from her edgy fingers, and stuffed her hands into the deep pockets of the robe. He walked through from what she presumed was the bedroom, and her heart stood still.

She loved him so much it was a physical pain. He'd changed into a pair of scuffed dark denims, and a black, soft cashmere sweater. He looked sexy as hell, but remote, grimly determined.

Her eyes met the dark enigma of his. She tried to read what was on his mind, but only when he spoke to her did she know. And when she did her heart twisted over and seemed to die, because surely this had to be the end.

'In spite of what I'd heard—that before we met you were more in Maclaine's bed than out of it—and in spite of what I'd actually seen, I tried to believe you spoke the truth when you told me you'd never had an affair with him,' Jake said bluntly, releasing her gaze as he walked over to the tray and poured from the elegant coffee-pot. 'I even managed it for a time. To believe you, that is.'

He passed her a cup, one brow lifting as she took it, the cup rattling on the saucer in her jittery hands.

Bella put it quickly down on a glass-topped table, and put herself on the cream hide-covered sofa. It was a case of sitting down before she fell down. Her legs had turned to water.

'But when I saw the two of you together tonight, I had to accept you could have lied. No—' he shook his head impatiently as she would have spoken in self-defence '—don't say a word. Hear me out.'

He was pacing the floor now, endlessly, the muscles of his body taut. 'And in that moment the whole world went black. But only for a moment. Trust came like a lightning bolt. I'd carried possessiveness too far, made too many false assumptions. Not waiting for answers, not believing them when they were given—as they were given when you told me you had nothing to do with the set-up in that mountain cottage. I knew I could trust you with my life.'

The pacing stopped. He faced her. There was a self-denigrating twist to his mouth she had never seen before. It astounded her.

'Can you ever forgive me for that lack?' he asked rawly. 'I failed you in every way that was important to you. I want us to start again. If you agree, things will be different, I promise.' He spread his hands, palms upwards, as if he held his life in them, offering all that he was to her.

'I've spent the last five days reorganising my working life. Delegating. Someone else can do the legwork. It's done. Sorted. My time will be spent with you and our family. If you still want my children.'

For the very first time she saw him unsure of himself, and she hated it. He shouldn't have to beg for what she freely wanted to give him. That he should subjugate his own needs, relinquish the cut and thrust of business, was a measure of his love for her.

She had only ever wanted his love, his trust. Everything else was irrelevant.

Happiness gushed through her like a wave breaking on rocks, and pure energy ran through her veins as she shot to her feet and covered the distance between them in jaunty strides.

'Now you listen.' She sounded breathless. 'It's my turn to come out with a few home truths.' She saw him flinch, every muscle tightening as if to prepare himself for a body blow, and couldn't bear it. Her hands went up to cup his beloved face, and she saw the vital spark of hope light up his eyes as she said throatily, 'Jake, I love you. Only you.'

She recognised the glow of intent deep in his eyes, and knew that in a moment she'd be held in his arms and there wouldn't be time for words, or any coherent thought left in her head. So she said with simple sincerity, 'I'm glad you sorted things out in your head and learned to trust me. I can't tell you how much that means to me. But, to put the record straight, whatever you've heard about my relationship with Guy isn't true. Just sly gossip, spread by people with nothing better to do.

'I've already explained how he looked out for me, and he was and is my friend. And, yes, his marriage did go through a rough patch, largely to do with Ruth's apparent inability to conceive. But he desperately wanted it to work because he'd been married before and it broke up. I don't know why; he didn't tell me.

'And, yes, we were seen around together. In my job there were a lot of functions and parties and stuff I had to attend. I had no one to escort me. I'd only had one man-friend, and that relationship turned out to be a disaster.'

He had taken her hands in his, his dark head bent as he pressed tiny, lingering kisses into her palms. She dragged in a helpful breath and gabbled on, not sure how much time she had left to get everything said before her mind blanked out beneath this sensual onslaught.

'He was a photographer who, I found out, thought bedding his female subjects one of the perks of his trade. If I thought very hard I might be able to remember his name! So Guy escorted me, and we ignored the gossip, and Ruth knew it wasn't true. And, tonight, he was trying to persuade me to take it up again—modelling. I told him no.'

He surely wasn't hearing a thing she said! His mouth had found the pulse points of the tender insides of her wrists. She didn't know how long she could hang onto her shaky control.

She dragged her hands away. 'Listen to me!' She backed away, putting the tenuous safety of a small distance between them. 'You walked in that night and found me in Guy's arms. And, yes, I guess it did look suspicious,' she agreed, seeing his body go tense again, his eyes take on that watchful, assessing look that told her he was weighing every word.

'He was comforting me. Being a friend. I'd been crying my eyes out over you, and he was telling me you'd have a good reason for being delayed.'

The watchful look had intensified. It made her bones shiver. But she'd allowed his lack of trust to ruin what had been left of their marriage before; she wouldn't let it happen again. Besides, hadn't he said he trusted her now?

To escape his eyes she turned and picked up her coffee, drained her cup. Her hands were completely steady now. She was, she decided, inhabiting the calm eye at the centre of the storm.

'You were to be home that Christmas Eve. I'd planned to make it special. You'd promised to be there, and, talking to you on the phone, I had the feeling that you wanted to get everything right again as much as I did. We both knew something was going wrong. But you didn't come. The meal had been prepared for hours. I'd put my glad rags on. My ears were sticking out on stalks listening for the sound of your key in the door. The phone rang—I thought it had to be you, telling me you'd been delayed, were on your way.'

She shivered, the memory of what had happened fraying her. 'It was Guy, phoning to wish us happy Christmas and spread his good news. Ruth had had her pregnancy confirmed. They were expecting twins. I wasn't listening,' she confessed tightly. 'I was bursting into sobs of disappointment because it wasn't you. And Guy and Ruth, like the good friends they are, came straight on round. Ruth was in the kitchen making fresh coffee and Guy was still trying to comfort me when you walked in, called me a vile name and walked out again. And didn't come back.

'I should have told you all this, waited around until you did decide to show up,' she whispered miserably. 'Got Guy and Ruth in to confirm it, if you couldn't believe me. But pride got in the way. You didn't trust me, and at the time I couldn't live with that. I didn't know then that you'd heard the old gossip about me and Guy, let alone believed it.'

She felt his arms go around her waist, and leant back against the strength of his body. Her voice was shaky as she told him, 'I want you to believe me now—not for my sake, but for yours. I don't want you to be hurt by doubt.'

'Sweetheart!' His voice was rough with emotion. He turned her in his arms. 'I hate myself for ever doubting you, for taking a later flight than I'd originally intended. But mistakes don't matter if we both learn from them. And I have learned, I promise.' His mouth claimed hers as he breathed, 'Oh, God, how I love you!'

She would treasure those words for the rest of her life, do her utmost to deserve them.

For the second time that evening he scooped her into his arms, but this time those black eyes were glittering with another emotion entirely, his intended destination far removed from the back of a cab. He dropped her on the big double bed and joined her, their limbs tangling instinctively, inevitably, no parting conceivable, not in their lifetime.

Bella awoke to a gentle rapping on the bedroom door. She yawned drowsily, delicately, like a cat, her body sated from passion.

She peered up at Jake through a tangle of black lashes. Sitting upright, propped against the pillows, his naked body gleamed like dull satin in the half-light of a winter's morning. His wide mouth was soft, tender, his eyes loving as he stroked the tumbled hair from her eyes then called 'Come.' His eyes held hers as he told her, 'Breakfast. Something special to mark a new beginning.' He got up and took the loaded tray from the room service waiter.

Scrambled eggs and smoked salmon. Bella forked up delicious mouthfuls as Jake poured champagne. He rejoined her amongst the wickedly rumpled sheets, holding his glass to hers, holding her eyes with his.

'Happy New Year, sweetheart.' His eyes glittered with sinful intent. 'Shall we start it as we mean to go on?'

Her heart quickened with immediate response. But there was something she really had to say. 'About your giving up work—you made it sound as if you were taking a very early retirement.' She couldn't ask that of him, let alone expect it. It was too much for him to sacrifice.

'I did some thinking,' she explained, idly running a fingertip across the rangy breadth of his chest. 'I could take a secretarial course and help you out on trips abroad. That way we'd be doing things together. I know how much work means to you. I can't see you staying put and twiddling your thumbs.'

'I have no intention of twiddling anything—well, certainly not my thumbs.' He grinned, planting a light kiss on the end of her nose. 'I grew up with an obsession about security. When I was a kid we seemed to have it all—a good home, everything any of us wanted, within reason. Dad owned a successful high-street hardware store, but he lost it, lost the house—everything. He found gambling on the stock market more exciting than selling screws and buckets.

'He killed himself soon after he'd been made bankrupt, and we were forced to live on the State, try to make sense of what had happened. I would have trusted that man to the ends of the earth. After what happened, the way he just left us to cope without him, mistrust came easily.

'I inherited Dad's fascination with the money markets,' he told her soberly. 'But, fortunately, not his capacity to make mistakes. But it was always there, at the back of my mind—the fear that I could come unstuck in a big way. It drove me to work harder and harder, determined that any family of mine would never have to suffer the way my father's did. It became an obsession. I didn't stay still long enough to register the fact that I'd got enough financial security to last several lifetimes.'

He rubbed his thumb over her lower lip. 'I've at last woken up to the fact that I want to make a life with you. A real life. Now, if you're still of the same mind, shall we see if we can begin to make that family of ours?'

The sinuous, seductive twist of her body against his was all the answer he needed.

EPILOGUE

'It's going to be a white Christmas,' Jake said, drawing the heavy brocade curtains, closing out the wintry landscape.

'Perfect!' Bella fixed the diaphanous fairy on the top of the tree and shuffled round on the stool she was standing on, holding out her arms to her beloved husband.

He helped her down, holding her close. In spite of her condition, in spite of his objections, she'd insisted on dressing the tree herself, as she did every year. She rested her head against his chest, twisting sideways a little because of her bulk. He felt the new life they were expecting in a few weeks' time kick against his body, and his hand went to hold her glossy dark head exactly where it was for a few more moments.

She was the most precious thing in his life, and her happiness spilled over and made his whole life bright.

A crash, a delighted squeal and a definite chortle alerted him to the fact that the second most precious thing in his life was up to mischief.

Incorrigible mischief—which was why they'd put him in his walker while the tree was being dressed, out of harm's way—or so they had thought.

'Bedtime, I think,' Jake stated, marching to the rescue, and Bella waddled after him, giggling as she retrieved the scattered brightly wrapped packages she'd stacked in a corner waiting to go under the tree after Jamie had gone to bed.

Starfish hands had found them. Jake gently ungripped the tiny fingers and lifted his son into his arms, where the grip was immediately transferred to his hair. 'I'll bath him,' he said. 'Put your feet up.'

'I'll make supper.'

'You'll put your feet up.'

Bossy, she thought, kissing her squirming son a fond goodnight and watching with love-drenched eyes as her husband walked from the room. She turned then, allowing the mellow homeliness of the room—one of over a dozen in this converted farmhouse—to soak into her.

Sometimes the perfection of her life overwhelmed her, filled her heart until she thought it would burst.

The perfect home, found only days after that ecstatic reconciliation. Deep in rolling countryside yet only an hour's drive from London.

The perfect child, and another to come.

The perfect husband. Oh, he still kept a finger decidedly on the pulse of his business affairs, but he worked from his study at the side of the house. It was a book-lined room, bristling with the technological monsters that allowed him to use his talents as an independent international financier, the head of a huge insurance company and a highly successful backer in the industrial and technological arenas of the world.

He still made time to share her life, care for her, taking a hands-on interest in helping her make a garden, manage the strip of woodland that bordered their very own lake.

The perfect husband, except for that bossy streak. Bella threw another log on the fire and went to make the supper, wondering if he'd like the gift she'd selected for him.

After a great deal of thought she'd decided on a chainsaw.

'Keep still, young Jamie. Kicking's fine when I'm teaching you the rudiments of football. Right now I'm trying to get you into this sleeping suit.'

Jamie talked back at him in baby talk, very fast and rather loud, and, mission accomplished, Jake squatted back on his heels and eyed his son. His son eyed him back then yawned, his dark eyes drooping.

Jake grinned and scooped him up, holding him close to his heart as he carried him out of a bathroom that looked as if a hurricane had struck. Somehow, when he took over Jamie's bathtime, it always ended up that way. And he got soaked.

As soon as he'd got him bedded down in the nursery he'd change and then make supper. He hoped Bella was doing as he'd told her—resting.

He was creeping carefully from the dimly lit nursery when Bella joined him.

'Asleep?'

He nodded. Their son had needed a whole bunch of stories, plus several not-very-tuneful renditions of lullabies—recalled out of desperation—before he'd consented to settle down.

Jake reached out and pulled her into the circle of his arms and Bella whispered, without a hint of contrition, 'Supper's almost ready. You'll just have time to change out of your wet things.'

'I thought I told you to rest,' he muttered gruffly as he helped her down the stairs, making sure she didn't trip. She had a mind of her own, and he loved her all the more for it. And he knew darn well he was only being allowed to help her down the staircase she used unaided twenty times a day because she liked him to touch her!

He wasn't what he'd call averse to it himself. As they successfully reached the foot of the stairs, just before he kissed her, he wondered if buying her a ride-on lawnmower had been the right choice of a gift for Christmas.

London's streets aren't just paved with gold—they're home to three of the world's most eligible bachelors!

You can meet these gorgeous men, and the women who steal their hearts, in:

NOTTING HILL GROOMS

Look out for these tantalizing romances set in London's exclusive Notting Hill, written by highly acclaimed authors who, between them, have sold more than 35 million books worldwide!

Irresistible Temptation by Sara Craven
Harlequin Presents® #2077
On sale December 1999

Reform of the Playboy by Mary Lyons
Harlequin Presents® #2083
On sale January 2000

The Millionaire Affair by Sophie Weston
Harlequin Presents® #2089
On sale February 2000

Available wherever Harlequin books are sold.

HARLEQUIN®
Makes any time special ™

Visit us at www.romance.net

HPNHG

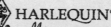

HARLEQUIN PRESENTS®

Seduction
SWEET ~~REVENGE~~

They wanted to get even.
Instead they got...married!

by bestselling author

Penny Jordan

Don't miss Penny Jordan's latest enthralling miniseries about four special women. Kelly, Anna, Beth and Dee share a bond of friendship and a burning desire to avenge a wrong. But in their quest for revenge, they each discover an even stronger emotion.
Love.

Look out for all four books in Harlequin Presents®:

November 1999
THE MISTRESS ASSIGNMENT

December 1999
LOVER BY DECEPTION

January 2000
A TREACHEROUS SEDUCTION

February 2000
THE MARRIAGE RESOLUTION

Available at your favorite retail outlet.

HARLEQUIN®
Makes any time special ™

HPSRS